Not Quite Miss Austen

Not Quite Miss Austen

A PREQUEL TO THE NOT QUITE SERIES

NOT QUITE SERIES

KIM GRIFFIN

Dedication

In memory of Miss Sherry (she's really a Mrs. but that's what I call her), one of my mom's dearest friends, a second mother to me since birth, and a Christ follower who loved well and ministered to many in the name of Christ. I will forever be thankful for her love and the impact she had on me and my family. She was there for my mom until the very end of her long journey with Alzheimer's and continued pouring out love on my family until her last days. She set such a beautiful example of friendship and service. Miss Sherry loved hummingbirds so look for one in the story, and she was known for the verses below.

For I know the plans I have for you, declares the LORD, plans for welfare and not for evil, to give you a future and a hope. 12 Then you will call upon me and come and pray to me, and I will hear you. 13 You will seek me and find me, when you seek me with all your heart.
Jeremiah 29:11-13 ESV

Contents

Chapter One

B*ut I could no more write a romance than an epic poem.*
-Jane Austen, Jane Austen's Letters

July 1955
London, England

Sipping tea in the reception room of a Belgravia, London, estate was not at all the way Margaret Elliot expected her interview with Corbyn Publishing to begin. Not that she minded. It was Darjeeling tea, and after so many years of rationing during the war, it felt like an extravagance.

Margaret took in the elegance of the room. It was formal with its chandelier, intricate trim and molding, and mahogany furnishings, but Mrs. Corbyn's friendly manner set her at ease.

She appreciated the time to gather her courage before her interview with Mr. Corbyn. She never knew what to say to new people. Her older siblings were much more suited to things like this. They were the outspoken ones in the family—even with perfect strangers. Margaret was most comfortable surrounded by her family, books, and a typewriter.

Her brother Arthur had secured the interview through his close friendship with Mr. Corbyn, so she'd imagined Mr. and Mrs. Corbyn were nearer to his age of thirty than her parents' ages, as Mrs. Corbyn appeared. It surprised her that someone so close to retirement age would embark on the complex task of starting a new publishing company.

She smiled up at Mrs. Corbyn. The older woman had clear blue eyes and white hair in a short, curly bob.

"Graham said you're hoping to publish books of your own. When did you start writing?" asked Mrs. Corbyn.

Margaret set her teacup back on the saucer and placed it on the round marble-topped side table as she gathered her thoughts. "I believe I wrote my first story when I was seven. At least that's how old my mum said I was when she found me writing under the willow tree in our back-yard—on some of her favorite stationery." She bit back a smile, recalling her mother's retelling of the story.

Mrs. Corbyn chuckled. "Well, I'm glad your interest brought you to us. I'm sure you'll be a help to Graham, and hopefully he can aid you in pursuing your dream of publishing your work. Your family means a great deal to us, and we are pleased to help you in any way we can, even if you don't work for us. Be assured of that. I think, however, that you and Graham will make a good team. He needs someone he can depend on in this new endeavor."

Something inside fluttered at the thought of seeing one of her stories bound into a book. "I'm optimistic—"

Before she finished her statement, the tall paneled wood door at the other end of the room swung open, and in the doorway stood the most handsome man Margaret had ever seen. Margaret tensed. He was tall, with blonde hair much lighter than hers, and he looked about her brother's age. She pondered that briefly, but it was his frown that unset-tled her.

"Graham, Miss Elliot is waiting for you," Mrs. Corbyn said as she stood and motioned toward Margaret.

Graham? This man was the one who founded the new publishing

company? Margaret looked between the two, stopped herself from asking the question on the tip of her tongue, and rose to greet him.

As he moved in her direction, his mouth lifted into a full grin, and his countenance changed. "Arthur's little sister. It's a pleasure to finally meet you. Your brother speaks so highly of you, yet somehow we've never met." He extended his hand, and she shook it.

"Thank you." She clenched her free hand behind her back and forced herself to say more. "He speaks highly of you as well."

"He's a good man and a good friend. Serving alongside him in the army was an honor and left me with a friend for life." He motioned to the door he had entered through. "Shall we? I have some things I'd like to discuss with you, and I'm sure you have questions." He held her gaze, and she noticed his blue eyes. They were a clear blue, just like Mrs. Corbyn's.

"Certainly."

"Would you like any tea, dear?" asked Mrs. Corbyn.

Graham glanced back. "No, thank you, Mother. But perhaps Miss Elliot would?"

"No, I've had plenty. Thank you, though." She noted the answer to her unspoken question and followed him into a library.

The smell of leather hit her as she entered. The room had wood-paneled walls, floor-to-ceiling bookcases filled with books, a seating area with a leather sofa and chairs, and a large wooden desk in the corner with a typewriter centered on it. It was simultaneously elegant and masculine.

Turning to the desk, she asked, "What shall I type for you?"

"Type for me?" He raised an eyebrow as he sat in a plush chair.

"Yes, my brother said you need someone to type. I assume you want to know how efficient I am? I type seventy words per minute and am ninety-eight percent accurate. I believe I will get faster. I've been continuing to increase my speed. Of course, that's all in my curriculum vitae, which I'm sure you've read." She clamped her mouth shut to keep from rambling further.

"I did look over it, and I do need someone to type, but I trust that your brother wouldn't send you to me and lie about your abilities." He stood back up and walked to the far side of the room before turning back to her. "Actually, I will let you show me what you can do. You'll find the paper in the top left drawer of the desk. I have a letter for you to type."

She nearly tripped as she hurried behind the desk and made herself comfortable. After loading a sheet of paper into the typewriter, she looked up expectantly.

"Ready?"

She held up a finger, typed in the date, then nodded.

"Mr. Hauser . . ." He paced across the room. "I am sorry to lose the pleasure of working with you." Moving in the opposite direction, he paused, shook his head, then continued his pacing. "Your book series has great potential. I wish you the best." He tapped a finger on his lip, and she caught a glimpse of the same frown she'd seen just before he greeted her. "But should you find yourself reconsidering your current decision, please know we will welcome you back. I have several ideas for marketing your book, and as I've said before, I believe we would make a good team." He pressed his lips together and nodded before adding, "Yours sincerely, Graham Corbyn. Corbyn Publishing. I think that's it." He moved behind the desk and rested a hand on the back of her chair while he leaned in to read the letter. "Perfect."

Margaret's heart skipped a beat as she caught a whiff of lemon, neroli, and possibly cedar. "I . . . if you'll give me the address, I'll add that at the top. I saved room." When he didn't respond, she turned her head and realized too late that they were nearly face to face. She blushed, then looked back at the typewriter.

"Right." He straightened and pulled a notepad from his desk. "I believe . . . yes, here it is."

He dictated the address. She quickly added it and handed him the letter.

"Excellently done, Miss Elliot. Thank you." He took the letter. "Why don't you join me in a more comfortable chair?" He gestured to the seating area on the other side of the room. "We can talk about the job and your salary."

Once they were seated, he explained the requirements of the position as his secretary and discussed how they might change as Corbyn Publishing grew from a startup company into something larger. He'd been running the company from his home for several months and had a few author contracts. There were also several others he'd already hired for various positions—an editor and three men to run the printing press and binding machines. "And you agree with our mission statement?"

"I do. I never thought there could be such a publisher, but it is exactly the type of place I want to work." She'd been driven by her faith in Jesus since becoming a Christian at age seven, and the thought of working for a company intent on putting out the works of Christian authors while pursuing publishing her own books was better than any job she could dream up.

"Wonderful. Then I'd like to offer you the job. To start, I want to offer five pounds a week. As you gain experience, we will reevaluate your wages. And of course, there is room for you to move up as the company grows. I will also include two tea breaks a day and lunch. Once we're working in the office building, I'll give you a lunch stipend and there will be a tea trolley, but here, the parlor maid will serve tea and lunch."

"So, there are plans for another location? I did wonder why you were housing a publishing company in a private home."

"The office is currently occupied, but their lease will be up shortly. It's only three blocks from here."

"I see," she said absently as she rolled the idea of five pounds around in her head. With Katie sharing her room in the boardinghouse, five pounds could work. Mrs. Fletcher was only charging them one pound each a week, and it included breakfast and dinner. "Will I get paid holidays, and how many?" She might be a dreamer, but she also had a practical side.

"Yes, two weeks' paid holidays per annum and all of the usual bank holidays."

Two weeks and bank holidays would provide ample opportunity to visit home, and for about half a pound, she could get round-trip coach fare. Likely, her family would come and visit her periodically too. The corner of her mouth drew up. She'd waited years for this dream to take shape.

"I'll take it." She thrust her hand out before her nerves got the best of her. "When do you want me to start?"

"I'd love for you to start tomorrow, and I imagine my mother would too, so she can stop acting as my secretary. But if you need a few days, I'll make do."

"If you really mean that, I'd like to start the day after tomorrow. My mum is here, and I'd like to spend some time with her before she returns . . . home." It felt strange calling the estate where her brother lived "home."

"Indeed, I meant it. Do you have any further questions?"

"No, sir. I'm excited to get started."

He dipped his head. "I'm pleased to have the honor of working with the dear sister of my good friend."

He stood and escorted her to the front door and reached out to shake her hand once more. "Miss Elliot, do call if you think of any questions before Wednesday."

His grip was firm and sent warmth up her spine. For a flash, she imagined staring up at him at the front of church with a pastor looking on. Where did that image come from?

"I'd also like to extend my sympathy to you and your family. I know these past months have been hard. Your father was a good man. I met him several times, and he always made me feel like part of the family. I appreciated that."

Though self-conscious, she flashed what she hoped was an appropriate smile, released his hand, and backed up. "Thank you. It has been hard, but we are adjusting. I-I'll see you Wednesday."

"Yes. Enjoy your time with your mother, Miss Elliot. Tell her hello for me. I'll see you promptly at nine in the morning on Wednesday. We close at five."

Margaret was already walking down the steps when he said his final words. Her mind was filled with competing thoughts, but she forced herself back to the present, stopped on the last step, and twisted to wave. "Yes, I'll see you then."

He returned her wave, but she didn't give him a chance to see the heat rising on her cheeks as she quickly turned back and continued on her way. She didn't dare mention that his mother had invited her to visit tomorrow with her own mother and friend. If he wasn't present, she would be all the happier to have the extra day to prepare to see him again.

By the time she reached the pavement, she heard the sound of the front door clicking shut, and she breathed a sigh of relief. She'd kept focused and calm for most of the interview, but there at the last, she'd reached her limit.

That image of the two of them—getting married—nearly did her already frayed nerves in. She'd only come here to work hard and glorify God through her writing. The job was a means to that end. She'd had no intention of marrying, but when she looked into Mr. Corbyn's eyes, she truly thought he was the man who might change her mind. It was an odd sensation, since they'd just met. Other than her brother's high opinion of him, she didn't know much about him.

She silently thanked God for the job and prayed that on Wednesday, he would help her overcome the anxiety she felt around Mr. Corbyn and keep her wits about her. She committed to doing everything in her power to keep any more errant husbandy thoughts away.

Birds chirping drew her attention to a park on the other side of the street, across from the house. She paused to examine the park and saw a couple of benches and a pretty lane for walking around an elegant garden. Her nervousness must have kept her from noticing such a lovely garden upon her arrival. She glanced back at Mr. Corbyn's stately home once more before turning in the direction of the Tube.

Margaret drew in a breath as a man narrowly missed colliding with her.

"Terribly sorry, miss. Are you quite alright?" he asked as he tipped his hat and held her gaze.

When he didn't turn away, she realized he was waiting for an answer. "Yes . . . I'm fine. Pardon me. I was distracted." She gestured in the direction she'd been gazing.

"No, it's my fault entirely. I wasn't watching where I was going. May I make it up to you? I can escort you somewhere and make sure another cad doesn't nearly run you off the pavement." His mouth pulled into a half smile that accentuated his black mustache.

He seemed kind, but his forwardness unnerved her. "Thank you for your offer, but I'll be sure to pay better attention the rest of the way." She took a step forward when she heard him call out.

"You were visiting my friend, Graham?"

Could she pretend she didn't hear and keep walking? No. It would likely get back to Mr. Corbyn that his new secretary was unsociable. She stopped again and turned. "You're friends with Mr. Corbyn?"

"Indeed, I am." He held out his hand. "Charles Sutton at your service."

She looked down at his hand and hesitated before shaking it. "Oh, I . . . I'm Margaret Elliot, his new secretary."

"Isn't he the lucky one, Miss Elliot? I hope to see you again in the future." He tipped his hat once more before turning and whistling as he approached Mr. Corbyn's home.

Her imagination ran wild as she walked away. His mustache resembled that of a much older man from the forties, yet he looked close to Mr. Corbyn's age. Maybe she could add an odd-looking character like him to the adventures of Mary and Sam in her Willowland series. She chuckled at the thought.

The image of the Corbyn home popped into her mind. Was it Mr. Corbyn's home? Or was it his mother's? She didn't see a ring on his finger, and it was a large home for a young single man. Maybe she could ask her brother in her next letter, if she could manage a tone that didn't sound too nosy.

She clutched the handle of her handbag and continued on her path to the Tube.

Chapter Two

Margaret leaned down to brush her fingers over the lavender flowers lining the pathway to Mrs. Fletcher's boarding-house in Ealing, where she and Katie were renting a room. The sweet scent filled the air, and she wondered how Mrs. Fletcher kept her garden so perfect in spite of the drought they'd been having over the summer. Spotting a watering can, she imagined the middle-aged woman spending hours tending to the garden.

She'd worried that moving to London would mean no more grass and flower-filled gardens, but between Mrs. Fletcher's home and the park in front of Mr. Corbyn's Belgravia home, she would have an abundance of God's beautiful creation in her life.

She lifted a fisted hand to knock on the door when she recalled that she lived here and could walk right in. It felt strange to walk into someone else's home, but she appreciated Mrs. Fletcher's hospitality. The only downside to living in Ealing was the forty-five minute commute on the Tube. Peeking back at the garden, she decided it was worth it to gain the pleasant environment at an affordable price.

Clinking china in the living room drew her attention the moment she opened the door, and she turned to follow the sound. Her mum and Katie were perched on the settee, and Mrs. Fletcher sat in an armchair next to them.

"Welcome home," Mrs. Fletcher greeted Margaret after glancing up. "Come join us for tea." She held up her teacup.

Margaret examined the platter of biscuits and scones on the coffee table, and her mouth watered. "Thank you."

"Have a seat and join us." Her mother pointed to the other armchair while Mrs. Fletcher retrieved a cup and saucer from the sideboard.

"How did it go, dear? Do you think you'll be happy working for Mr. Corbyn? Is the job satisfactory?"

"Yes, he and his mum are both lovely people. And before I forget, Mrs. Corbyn invited you over before you leave. But back to the job. There's an editor I haven't met. Mr. Corbyn said she's working from home until their real office is ready. For now, I'll be working in their home."

"That's unusual, but it is a lovely estate, and I'm sure it will be pleasant to work in."

"It is beautiful. He said he has an office lined up but is waiting for the current tenant to move out."

"I suppose those things happen when you first start a company."

"So tell me about the Belgravia home." Katie grinned and shifted to the edge of the settee.

"I'll leave you ladies to socialize. If you'll excuse me." Mrs. Fletcher rose to leave. "Enjoy your tea."

After Mrs. Fletcher left the room, Katie continued her entreaty. "How does it compare to Ashe Park? In the interiors."

"Oh, Katie." Margaret paused to recall the rooms she saw. "It is very grand. The entrance has an elegant carved wooden staircase that goes up several floors, and all of the ceilings on the ground floor are very high and have elaborate molding." She glanced at her mother. "I had tea with Mrs. Corbyn in the reception room, which was filled with mahogany antiques, then Mr. Corbyn"—her gaze flitted to Katie, and Katie raised a brow—"had me join him in the library for my interview. It was exactly as you would imagine, with the floor-to-ceiling dark wood bookcases. All very elegant, though not nearly as large as Ashe Park."

"I'm thrilled that you've found a place you think will make you happy, though I will miss you." Her mother pulled a handkerchief from her pocket and dabbed her eyes. "I'm not trying to make you feel bad, but you are loved, and it's hard to believe my youngest will be gone."

"Oh, Mum." Margaret rushed to her mother's side and squeezed in between her and Katie to wrap an arm around her. "I don't want to make you sad." The past six months of her mother mourning her father's death after thirty-one years of marriage, then leaving her parsonage home of nearly twenty years to move in with her son and his family, had taken its toll on Mrs. Elliot. Margaret didn't want to add to her troubled heart.

"No. Don't mind my tears, dear. I suppose they are just as much happy tears as they are sad ones. I want you to do what God has called you to. Your father would be so proud. And I do believe it will help you to not be in the shadow of your sisters. They can be a bit . . . much at times."

"You know it's never bothered me. I love my sisters and have always enjoyed sitting back and watching their antics."

"I suppose that is partly why you're so good at writing. You are keen in your observations, and I have always enjoyed the depth of your insight. You are wise for one so young. Anyway, know I will miss you, my dear."

"You can visit, and I will try to visit you as often as possible."

"I don't expect you to feel the need to come visit often, though I will love it when you do."

"Thank you, Mum. I love you, and I'll miss you too."

"You made a face when you mentioned Mr. Corbyn," Katie stated once they were tucked into their beds in the dark. "What's he like? He's your brother's friend—I wouldn't think he would be that bad. What was his wife like? You never said."

"Because Mrs. Corbyn isn't his wife."

"No?"

"No. She's his mum. She was helping him out until he hired a secretary. And there's nothing wrong with him." Far from it.

Margaret heard shuffling before the lamp came on. She blinked up at Katie.

"So why did you make the face? Is he married?"

Margaret's face heated. "You ask a lot of questions." She recalled getting a glimpse of his left hand. "I don't think he's married. There was no ring."

"Is he handsome?"

Margaret's face heated again. "Katie, stop." She knew what her friend was getting at. "Yes, he's handsome, and perhaps *if* I ever marry, it would be to someone like him." There. She said it. Sort of.

"Why not him?"

"He's my employer, he's probably ten years older than me, and he's my brother's good friend. You know my thoughts on marriage, and I doubt he would ever consider someone like me. Besides, I barely know him. Maybe I'll discover something awful once I get to know him."

Katie's lips turned up. "Maybe you can introduce me. I'm here to find a man to marry. There are so many more to choose from here than in Steventon."

"You may have an opportunity tomorrow, but please don't chase after him." Katie would likely turn his head with her fun and bubbly personality, and deep down, Margaret worried she would be jealous of her friend if he did show interest.

"So you do think you could marry him? Don't worry, I won't chase after him. I was only trying to get your reaction."

Margaret let out another sigh. "We've only just met, and I have things I'm here to do." She thought back to the image of him at the altar. "I'll make this brief confession, but then I don't want to talk about it again."

Katie's eyes opened wide.

"As we were saying goodbye, he shook my hand, and I had a flash of an image of the two of us before the altar at a church with a minister before us. We were dressed to get married."

A gasp escaped Katie's open mouth, but she quickly clamped it shut.

"It was just a flash of a thought, but it does have me thinking that maybe God does intend for me to marry after all, in spite of John, and Mr. Corbyn might be the man God has for me. Much further into the future, of course. He *is* in the literary field, and more importantly, he must love God if he's going to all this trouble to start a publishing company for Christian authors." Confusion swirled in Margaret's mind about her feelings towards Mr. Corbyn and the idea of marrying at all, and she wasn't ready to sort through them.

"Now—tell me about your day at Selfridges. Any handsome men there? And do you think it will be a good job for you?"

"Yes and yes," Katie answered. "And I, too, requested to start work on Wednesday, so we can tour the town tomorrow like we planned. From what you said, I'm guessing we're going to the Corbyns' home tomorrow."

"We are." Margaret arched one eyebrow at Katie pointedly. "Mrs. Corbyn said we could come by about nine-thirty. I'm thinking we can visit there for a bit before walking to Buckingham Palace to watch the changing of the guard. It's only a few minutes away. We'll drop my mum off at the train station midday so she can get home at a decent hour, then we'll have the afternoon to explore."

Katie sighed. "I can't believe we're really doing this. We've talked about moving to London for months. Do you think you'll feel homesick?"

"It's hard to say. Right now, I'm just so excited about finally getting my chance to work at a publishing house that I don't care where I am. We do need to make sure we can save money to visit home regularly, though. Even if I'm not homesick, I will still want to visit everyone. Actually—" Margaret pressed a finger to her chin. "I'll miss the green spaces—especially my favorite willow tree."

"I didn't think of that. Where will you write now? I know that's your favorite spot."

"And where I come up with my best ideas." She recalled the park across the street from the Corbyns' home. "But there is a pretty little park across the street from where I'll be working. Maybe I can fold a blanket into a bag to take to work and eat my lunch out there sometimes."

"That sounds delightful. If I have a weekday off, maybe I can join you. I'll bring my copy of Northanger Abbey and read while you write." Katie tapped the book on the nightstand.

"I'd love that."

"See. We're already adjusting."

Chapter Three

From a settee in the Corbyn's reception room, Margaret sat next to Katie and watched as Mrs. Corbyn and her mother chatted. The two women had met a few times before because of their sons, but their conversation had the familiarity of two people who had been close for years.

"Thank you so much for your encouraging letters. They have meant the world to me over these past few months," Margaret's mother said.

"It is a small thing, but I am glad they've been encouraging to you," replied Mrs. Corbyn.

"Knowing that you have been through the same thing makes your advice and words so much more meaningful. Those first few months, I felt so lost. Even now I sometimes wake up expecting to see my husband next to me, or hear him call out that he is preparing his sermon for Sunday." Margaret's mother's hand went to her chest, and Mrs. Corbyn touched her shoulder.

"May I pray for you?"

"Yes . . . Thank you." Her mother choked out her words and bowed her head.

Margaret and Katie followed suit as Mrs. Corbyn prayed over her mother and asked God to strengthen, comfort, and equip her for the days ahead.

"Thank you. I'm sure it is your prayers and those of others that have carried me through."

"You are quite welcome. I only wish we had more time together. Are you sure you won't stay an extra day? The three of you could dine with me and Graham for dinner."

"I do appreciate the offer and am disappointed to have missed him, but I promised my son that I would be home this evening so I can watch the children while he and his wife attend an event."

"I assure you, Graham will be disappointed to have missed you. This appointment popped up, and he could not reschedule it for another time."

Margaret found herself disappointed at the news but didn't have time to examine why, because Katie pinched her leg.

When she turned to whisper her frustration into Katie's ear, she found her friend with a raised eyebrow and a smirk.

Margaret shook her head, and Katie leaned in to whisper, "We will definitely be talking later." She smoothed her dress, glanced around the room, and whispered again. "It is just as lovely as Ashe Park. You've made out quite well to get to work at a place like this."

"Though it's only our temporary office." Perhaps Katie would soon forget about her reaction to hearing Mr. Corbyn discussed.

"Still. Enjoy it while it lasts."

Heavy footsteps drew their attention to the doorway, and Margaret wondered if the footman had a message for Mrs. Corbyn, but when the door opened, her eyes met Mr. Corbyn's instead. An unmistakable flutter filled her. So much for keeping her errant thoughts at bay.

He smiled and nodded at Margaret before turning to her mother. "Mrs. Elliot. It's so good to see you. I was worried I'd miss you." He took wide strides as he crossed the floor and leaned down to shake her mother's hand. "It's been too long since I've seen you—" He opened his mouth to say more, before shutting it and shaking his head. "I'm truly sorry for your loss. Like I told Margaret yesterday, he was a good man, and I was honored to know him." He glanced across the room at Margaret.

"I appreciate your kind words, and I certainly appreciated the flowers you and your mother sent. They were beautiful," said Mrs. Elliot.

"I wish we could have alleviated your pain in a more useful way, but from our own experience, we know that will take time. Don't we, Mum?"

Mrs. Corbyn looked up, and sadness lurked behind her usually smiling eyes. "Indeed we do." Glancing at Margaret's mother, her eyes brightened. "But enough about sad things. They are leaving soon to watch the changing of the guard before Mrs. Elliot returns home."

"Wonderful. Have you seen it before?" He glanced between Katie, Margaret, and her mother, who all shook their heads. Walking to the settee, he extended a hand to Katie. "Pardon me. I'm sorry for not introducing myself right away. I gather you're Margaret's friend and room-mate? I'm Graham Corbyn."

Katie's eyes lit up. "I'm Katie O'Neil."

"Pleased to meet you, Katie O'Neil. I should have guessed at your Irish heritage from your hair."

Katie's cheeks turned pink, making her freckles stand out, and she smiled while twisting a lock of her curly red hair.

"I'll let you ladies finish your visit in peace. Some of us have to work." He looked pointedly at Margaret and bit back a grin. "Others of us took a day off."

Turning back to Margaret's mother, he said goodbye before exiting to his study.

Margaret continued waving to the train until she could no longer see it as it pulled away from Victoria Station.

"Now." Katie tugged Margaret's hand and pulled her toward the exit. Her mouth twisted into a grin. "You failed to mention just *how* handsome your Mr. Corbyn is."

Margaret rolled her eyes. "He's not *my* Mr. Corbyn, and I told you he's handsome."

"Oh, Margaret. One of these days, you're going to move past John Sinclair."

"How I feel has nothing to do with John Sinclair."

"If you say so," Katie said in a sing-song voice while tugging her until they stood at the bus stop.

They didn't wait long before the bus arrived, and they began their trek to the London Zoo.

"I feel like we're on a sightseeing bus. We've made so many stops," Katie complained after forty minutes of travel.

"At least on the bus, we can see the sights. Look, I think that's the zoo!"

After exiting the bus, they turned a corner and found a street lined with shops.

"Look!" Katie pointed to a beauty shop.

"Do you like the hairstyles in their display?" The mannequin heads displayed the latest styles. Margaret had seen some in magazines.

"I do." Katie clasped her hands together. "Margaret, we should get our hair cut and set! Wouldn't it be wonderful to start our new jobs with modern, grown-up hairstyles?"

"I . . ." She tilted her head and examined the mannequins once more. They did look nice.

"I know your brother gave you some pocket money. What better way to spend it than starting your job off right by looking professional? The zoo isn't going anywhere if we don't have time to go today."

"Okay. You've convinced me. Let's do it." Before she could talk herself out of it, Margaret led the way into the beauty shop.

After discussing styles with the hairdresser, she decided on a short bob with loose waves. Once it was completed, she admired the new look in the mirror before the hairdresser spun the chair and held up another small mirror so she could see the back.

"What do you think?" asked the beautician.

Margaret touched her honey-blonde hair. It was shorter than what she was used to, but it did look elegant.

"I like it." She grinned, and truly meant it.

"Don't we look smart?" Katie turned to Margaret and patted her simplified victory rolls.

"I think I can do this on my own with the right styling products," Margaret said once they'd paid and were standing outside of the shop.

"See! You'll be so glad you did this. We may be young, but I want to be taken seriously."

Nodding, Margaret thought about how her life could change over the next few months and even years as she made progress in the publishing world. She really was living the life she'd dreamed about.

After leaving the salon, they made their way to the zoo. A sign at the entrance recommended a special exhibit of American birds in the aviary, so once they paid, they made a direct path to the aviary. Margaret and Katie were both intrigued by the hummingbirds. Neither of them had ever seen anything like the little birds. Margaret focused on one hovering over a honeysuckle blossom. Its iridescent feathers reflected the sunlight coming through the screen above as its pointed beak poked into the trumpet-shaped flower. Its wings fluttered so fast, she couldn't make out their shape but heard a distinct humming that she guessed gave them their name.

She looked up at Katie with a smile, still not believing they finally lived in London. Tomorrow would be the start of something wonderful.

Chapter Four

"Corbyn Publishing, printing books that change the world. This is Margaret Elliot. How may I help you today?" Margaret said cheerfully into the phone and grinned as she took down the information from the caller.

She'd added the part about printing books that change the world because of Mr. Corbyn's mission to do that very thing by getting the work of Christian authors out into the world. When she'd asked Mr. Corbyn if she could add it when answering the phone, he'd mulled it over and decided it was perfect. He even asked if she would consider letting them use it for advertisements, and he would pay her a bonus. Her first day couldn't have started any better.

First thing in the morning, Mr. Corbyn had gone over several jobs for Margaret to do before he hurried out to a meeting with a potential author. Mrs. Corbyn had been gone for her volunteer work when Margaret arrived, so after he left, she was alone except for the house staff.

Her stomach growled, and she looked at her watch. It was about lunchtime. Mr. Corbyn had told her to let the parlor maid know what time she wanted to eat, and she'd requested her meal at one.

Margaret pushed her chair back from the desk and stretched. She'd kept so busy with the backlog of letters, brochures, and other paperwork he had been saving for her to type that she'd hardly noticed the passage of time.

Just as she stood to look for the parlor maid, Gretchen, the woman herself, entered the room. "Cook said your lunch is ready. Would you like me to serve you in the dining room?"

Margaret thought about the lovely space with all of its formal furniture and enormous table but didn't relish eating there alone. "Actually, would it be possible for me to have it put in a basket for a picnic? And if you know of a spare cloth I could lay on the ground to picnic on, I would really appreciate it."

"Of course, ma'am. We have just the thing for that." Gretchen's face lit up as she spoke.

"Thank you, Gretchen." Margaret hugged herself when the maid left the room. She'd been eyeing the park across the street on her way in and hoped for the opportunity to go out for breaks and sit under a tree. The weather was warm, but in the shade, it would be perfect. She'd just happened to bring her notebook with her latest Willowland story and also a small Bible. It wouldn't be exactly like her writing spot at home, but it would make a pleasant substitute.

Minutes later, she'd found the perfect tree in the park to spread the picnic cloth under. Leaning back against the tree, she breathed in the fresh warm air. "Thank you, God," she whispered.

Presently, she was the only one in her section of the park. A couple had left the park hand-in-hand just as she was walking in.

Margaret laid out the food Gretchen gave her. Cook said it was no trouble when Gretchen told her about the change, and she had the perfect cold dishes to serve instead of the hot meal she'd prepared for the day. Gretchen insisted the hot meal wouldn't go to waste. The new meal consisted of a green salad and coronation chicken with rice. Margaret had heard of the coronation chicken dish, which had been created for Queen Elizabeth II's coronation two years earlier. She couldn't wait to taste it.

After preparing her plate, she took a bite of the chicken dish. *Mmm.* The creamy sauce was slightly sweet and had an earthy tang she could tell came from curry and tomato sauce, but she wasn't sure what else made up the flavor. It was delicious, and she wondered if the cook would share her recipe.

Quickly finishing her meal, Margaret pulled out her Bible. She'd been reading through the Psalms and loved the way the psalmists poured out their anguish to God just as easily as they poured out their praise. Today's psalm, Psalm 96, was an uplifting one.

She laid aside her Bible and closed her eyes, thanking God for the perfect start to her job and the many blessings he'd shown her.

A shadow fell over her, and when she opened her eyes, she found Mr. Corbyn standing over her with a smile on his face and a raised brow.

"I returned to join you for lunch, and Miss Hoffman said you were lunching in the park. Does the house feel too stuffy for you, Miss Elliot?"

It took Margaret a second before she recalled that Miss Hoffman was Gretchen. "Oh, no. It was such a beautiful day, and no one was there to eat with me, so I couldn't pass it up."

"And do a little reading?" He gestured to her Bible and notebook, and she followed his gaze.

"I enjoy spending time with God and writing outside. At home, my favorite spot is under a willow tree growing next to a pond." When she looked back up, he was staring at her. A flutter stirred inside.

His smile brightened. "Pardon me for staring, but I'm still adjusting to your new look. I almost didn't recognize you as I passed. I must say, it makes you look so . . . professional."

"Professional?" That didn't sound like something he would equate with attractive, and she felt self-conscious. She tugged at her hair, still getting used to the shorter look and feel. "Is that your way of saying I look boring?"

"Not at all. It looks very modern and elegant on you. Very . . . nice." He shook his head as if waking from a daze, and color rose to his cheeks. "What were we speaking of before?" He looked down at her Bible again. "Oh, yes. You were reading your Bible. Spending time with God is a worthwhile occupation. May I join you?" He pointed to the picnic cloth.

"Of course." Margaret nodded.

"What are you reading?" he asked as he sat.

"I was just now reading Psalm 96. I love the phrase 'ascribe to the Lord' that's used in it. One verse says, 'Ascribe to the Lord the glory due his name; bring an offering, and come into his courts!' Isn't that just beautiful? So many of the psalms turn our hearts to God. Another verse says, 'Let the field exult, and everything in it! Then shall all the trees of the wood sing for joy.'" She waved her hand at the surrounding trees. "Can't you just imagine the trees in heaven singing for joy? I've begun going through Romans this week too. I read Romans in the morning and evening, with the Psalms as a pick-me-up during the day."

"You read your Bible every day?"

"I do. There are occasions I only have the time for a few verses, but I find I have a better attitude and am more focused when I spend more time with the Lord in his Word and in prayer."

"I can't imagine a better way to bring focus to one's life. And Romans is a rich book, filled with the essentials of the faith. I'd love to discuss what you're learning in it another time." His smile curved up on one side. "But surely, Arthur's favorite sister's attitude is always as it should be, even before she opens God's Word."

Margaret giggled and shook her head. "I don't know what Arthur told you, but I doubt it's that I'm perfect. I may be the quiet one among my siblings, but I'm strong-willed and passionate about what I believe in. I have to work to make sure that what I am passionate about are things that please the Lord and not what I came up with in my fanciful imagination."

"Your fanciful imagination?"

"Surely Arthur mentioned that? I'm the sister who—" Maybe she shouldn't incriminate herself. And why was she freely speaking to her boss—who she barely knew and secretly wanted to impress—about what some considered a flaw? Did she so closely associate him with her dearly loved brother that it erased her usual reserve?

"Do go on. I want to know about your fanciful imagination."

She felt her face heat but forced herself to continue. "I'm the sister who creates imaginary worlds . . . and friends. There's an age gap between me and the others, so I made my own fun through the years. Though they were never mean-spirited in their teasing, my siblings often teased me about talking to myself."

"Other worlds. Are these other worlds in the books you want to publish?"

She nodded. "One of them is. It's the Willowland series I'm writing."

"Hmm." He tapped his chin and leaned in. "Tell me more about your series and its world."

"I was influenced by C. S. Lewis's *The Lion, the Witch, and the Wardrobe*. I fell in love with that book, and I believe that it is what influenced me the most to write. Not that I have anywhere near the power over words that he does. Despite being from the hometown of Jane Austen, my imagination has always been bent towards fantastical worlds, and I really can't see myself ever writing romance. I'm certainly not experienced enough to write about it." She clamped her mouth shut. What was it about this man that drew out her deepest secrets?

"You're holding back. You can tell me more about your writing. I deal in fanciful stories, remember?"

Some people thought her imagination was out of control and silly. Margaret gathered her courage. "When I read Lewis's book, it gave me the confidence to write that type of story. My Willowland series is based around the lives of two young children—Mary and Sam. They live in modern times, but when they sit under the willow tree in their field, they dream of adventures in a world in the clouds. When it happened the first time, they recounted their stories and realized they had exactly the same dream."

"What an intriguing setup for a series. What age is it for?"

"It's aimed at older primary schools, but I hope that, like C. S. Lewis's book, adults will appreciate the books too."

"I'll do everything in my power to help you accomplish that goal."

"Thank you." She dipped her head. Although publishing her own books was her reason for working at a publishing company, she suddenly felt selfish for putting her manuscripts forward. Yet how would she ever become a successful author if she wasn't willing to promote her own books?

At a loss for what to say next, she glanced at her watch. "Oh dear, it seems my lunch break is over."

"I'm sorry for intruding on your time. You had wanted to write more about your Mary and Sam, I imagine."

He scooped up the basket sitting beside her and reached for her hand.

"It's fine, I—" Sparks shot through her hand, and her thoughts jumbled. "It's fine," she repeated as she shook her head.

Mr. Corbyn chuckled as he helped her up and took the picnic cloth from her hand.

When her previous thoughts returned, she spoke up. "I'm more worried about you. Did you miss your own lunch while looking for me?"

"Don't worry. I'll have Miss Hoffman bring me something to eat while I'm working."

He deposited her at the desk he'd set up for her on one side of the library. He'd assured her that both doors to the room would stay open for decorum. She'd thought she'd feel anxious working in the same room with him, but as she discovered with their relaxed conversations that afternoon, he had a way of setting her at ease. It also helped that she'd banished thoughts of marrying him . . . mostly. Getting Katie to stop bringing it up would be another challenge.

Staying busy with the work before her helped keep her mind off of the man sitting feet away. He had enough typing alone for several days of work.

"It's about that time, Miss Elliot."

Mr. Corbyn's voice drew Margaret from her typing. "Hmm?"

"It's the end of your workday. Five thirty."

Margaret glanced at her watch. "Oh, it is." Her work kept her thoroughly engrossed, despite the simplicity of it. "I think I can just make the next bus if I hurry." She quickly tidied her desk and gathered her things.

"No need. Why don't I drive you? I have a dinner meeting in that direction and will have plenty of time to make it if I drop you off first."

Surely it wouldn't be right for him to drive her home. She searched her mind for some excuse, but nothing solid came to the forefront. "I hate for you to bother with me."

"Like I said, I'm going that way. It's no trouble and will save you the bus fare."

"Okay." She could do this. "Thank you."

"Great. It will give me a chance to get to know you better and chat with you about your study of Romans."

Peace settled inside of Margaret. She loved to talk about God's Word. Maybe it wouldn't be so awkward riding with Mr. Corbyn.

<h1 style="text-align:center">Chapter Five</h1>

Margaret's first couple of days of work flew by. Mr. Corbyn hadn't taken her home again, and they'd settled into a routine at work. He did surprise her the day after driving her home by saying he wanted to start the mornings at work with Bible study. He said it wasn't required, and his mum would join them in the study while they were working at the Belgravia home. He planned to continue when they moved to the new office.

The idea thrilled her, and she was even more excited to find out he wanted to study Romans first. He said Romans was filled with so much essential doctrine that he couldn't think of a better book to start with. After asking Margaret about her process of studying, he decided they would first read through all of Romans to get an overview. She'd found that method to be helpful before going back through it more slowly and intensively.

They decided which verses to read on their own, and when they met the following morning, they began by discussing what they found in their separate studies. Though it was only their first official study, they had a lively discussion. Margaret was surprised at how well Mr. Corbyn knew his Bible. She didn't know many men not in full-time ministry who did. Even her brother, the son of a minister, didn't have as much knowledge as Corbyn seemed to. She'd always enjoyed learning, and Mr.

Corbyn challenged her to dig deeper through their discussion. His mother's knowledge was fairly solid, too, and she wondered if that was where he gained his love of scripture.

Later that day, Mr. Corbyn quietly worked at his desk when he wasn't on the phone or working directly with her on something. She struggled to keep her thoughts and eyes from drifting to him. He looked so handsome as he examined manuscripts and did other work at his desk. Presently, he was speaking on the phone. She'd been successfully blocking out most of his conversations so she could work, but this time, his voice began to rise.

"Mrs. Brown, I promise I will do everything in my power to ensure you succeed while maintaining the strong faith aspect of your books as we promote you. Are you sure that—"

Margaret glanced over, and he was clenching a pen while writing intently. He frowned, and it reminded her of the look on his face the first time she saw him, just before her interview.

"No, ma'am. I—" His voice softened. "Yes, I understand. I'm sorry too."

He slammed the receiver down and dropped the pen to the desk, huffing out a long breath before burying his face in his hands.

Unsure of what to do, Margaret watched on silently. When he picked up the pen and began to write, she decided it was time to speak up.

"Mr. Corbyn, how may I help?"

"What?" His head snapped in her direction, and his brow furrowed. "Miss Elliot. I'd forgotten you were there."

"Is there anything I can do to help?" she repeated.

He shook his head and mumbled under his breath before speaking more clearly. "No." With no further response, he looked back down at the paper and continued writing.

The cold look on his face and snap of his voice left her at a loss for words. She'd not seen this side of him before, and she wasn't sure what to make of it. Looking down at her own work, she tried to refocus, but her mind was fuzzy.

When she finally gained the courage, she looked up to see him reading his Bible. That was a good sign and also a reminder for her to pray. She silently asked God to help her handle her feelings of rejection, to help Mr. Corbyn, and to show her if there was anything she could do to help.

After her prayer, she was surprised at how well she refocused on her work.

"Miss Elliot?" Mr. Corbyn's voice broke through her concentration. "Yes?"

"I'm sorry for the way I acted toward you earlier. You were trying to help, and I callously brushed you off." He paused and seemed to think. "And yes, you can help. For starters, you can pray. Pray for my . . . our company. As I said before, I truly believe God called me to start a publishing house for Christian authors and books that point to God. Some things have been happening . . . and I believe the company is coming under spiritual attack."

Spiritual attack. It sounded so ominous. But it shouldn't surprise her. "My father often said that when we are following God's call, we shouldn't be surprised if Satan throws everything he can at us to thwart it."

"Those are wise words. Most aspects of starting this new business have come easily after my previous work at Hall & Wright. But when I worked for someone else, it was simpler to handle it when . . . things didn't work out how I'd hoped."

"That makes sense." She preferred for him to confide in her the specific problem he had but understood he might not want to tell a secretary the details of the business.

That afternoon, Mr. Corbyn had her type a letter to Mrs. Brown. The letter's message gave her the impression that his problem was authors backing out before signing with him. It was clear Mrs. Brown had backed out herself. How devastating for someone just starting a new company.

The phone rang. Margaret had her greeting down but worked to keep it from sounding robotic. "Corbyn Publishing, printing books that change the world. This is Margaret Elliot. How may I help you today?"

"Hi, Margaret. This is Frances. I'm sure Graham told you about me. Is he available to talk?"

The woman on the line spoke quickly and authoritatively but

sounded sophisticated and young. From the informal way she addressed Mr. Corbyn, she also knew him well. Funny that Mr. Graham had not mentioned a woman named Frances. Or maybe it wasn't funny at all. Perhaps she would be better off not knowing who this woman was who called him by his first name.

"Just a minute, please." Margaret stepped over to Mr. Corbyn and whispered, "There's a woman named Frances on the phone who has asked to speak with you. Would you like the phone?"

His hard look lifted into a smile. "Of course! Thank you!"

Margaret returned to her desk and moved the phone from her desk to his. His improved countenance had her wondering who the woman was.

"Good afternoon, Frances. Just calling for an afternoon check-in?" He paused, then chuckled.

Margaret didn't miss how his shoulders relaxed and he leaned back in his chair.

"Yes. Mm-hmm. I don't think so."

Returning to the paper in front of her, Margaret determined not to allow herself to keep looking at him in her peripheral vision. Ignoring his conversation was harder.

"Not until after lunch. Yes, I'll see you then." He stopped to listen. "Ha ha." He mock chuckled. "You too."

She heard the receiver hit the base before Mr. Corbyn said, "Miss Elliot. Wednesday after lunch, Frances Fairfax will come by, and I'd like you to meet her. She's our editor."

Strangely, Margaret felt relieved at the thought. "Wonderful. I look forward to it."

"Good. We're lucky to have her. She doesn't have to work and stays plenty busy with her volunteering, but because of our relationship, she's willing to do this until I grow the company and can bring on a full-time editor and more as needed."

And just like that, her heart sank. She'd been telling herself not to think of him as more than a friend, and yet she already felt a loss at his declaration. *Their relationship.*

"That's so good of her." She added more cheer to her voice than she felt.

When she turned back to her work, she felt silly for letting her thoughts get carried away. She was no longer a little girl and needed to better separate her fantasy life from reality. Maybe she should write a romance novel after all. At least that would be an outlet for her recent line of thought about a certain boss.

A knock on the door drew her attention away from Mr. Corbyn until he spoke. "Come in."

"Sir, Mr. Sutton is here to see you," the butler announced. "Should I send him in?"

The name sounded familiar.

"Certainly. Thank you, Jones," Mr. Corbyn replied before turning to Margaret. "I hope you don't mind. He's a friend of mine. I'll just introduce you to him, then we'll move to the reception room so we don't disturb you."

"Thank you. That's thoughtful."

"It's the least I can do since we're working in cramped quarters."

Margaret chuckled as she took in the room. It hardly qualified as cramped, but it did make conversations with others awkward.

Mr. Corbyn quirked a brow and opened his mouth, but the sound of the door opening had them both turning in the other direction.

"Fancy seeing you again!"

The man Margaret met on her way out from her interview entered the room, hat in hand, and she recalled him introducing himself as Charles Sutton.

"You two have met?" Mr. Corbyn stood and looked between Margaret and Mr. Sutton.

"Indeed we have. And I must say, I'm quite glad you've found someone as lovely as Miss Elliot here."

She felt heat rise to her cheeks. And how did he remember her name?

Mr. Sutton gave her an encouraging nod. "I'm glad to see you're settling in well. I suppose he's treating you alright?" Mischief danced in his eyes.

"Oh, yes. Thank you."

"Alright, Charles. I'll not have you embarrassing my new secretary with your flirtations. She's wonderful, and I am lucky to have her. Miss Elliot, pay no attention to half of what Charles says."

"What about the other half?" she wondered out loud.

"Sometimes he does actually have some ideas worth listening to."

The side of Mr. Sutton's mouth quirked up. "I am rather brilliant, aren't I?"

Mr. Corbyn shook his head and led Mr. Sutton to the parlor before turning back. "Feel free to pop in if you need anything. Or maybe to come and save me." He chuckled as he left.

"I heard that," Mr. Sutton called out from the next room.

Margaret was left with her thoughts and plenty of work to distract her.

"So you see, it's a good thing," Margaret told Katie that night after telling her about the woman named Frances.

Lying flat on her back, she stared at the ceiling from her spot on the bed and hoped her words would become reality.

"I don't know that I agree it's good. And Frances Fairfax—the name sounds pretentious."

"Don't judge her. You don't know her, and neither do I. She sounded very sophisticated over the phone." Margaret recalled the lilt of her voice. "But really, I shouldn't have let my mind get carried away with ideas of him in the first place. When I first had thoughts about him being the man I married, I honestly still thought of it as a faraway occurrence, if at all. Yet somehow between those first thoughts and this morning, my mind formed a different plan. Now I have a firm reason to stop that train of thought. Not that I didn't before. And I should have known he would be in a relationship. He must be close to my brother's age, and my brother has been married for eight years and has three children already."

"You're right. I'm sorry for pushing it. But even if he's not the one, it's a good sign that you're thinking about relationships again."

Margaret rolled her eyes. "Not really. This was just a fluke."

"He is a nice guy, so I don't blame you for being infatuated with him."

"I'm not infatuated . . . at least, I don't think so." She yawned and closed her eyes, trying not to think of the tall, handsome publishing entrepreneur.

"Let's focus on happier things, like your birthday tomorrow," Katie said as she switched off the lamp.

"Mm-hmm." A much safer subject for her dreams.

Chapter Six

Margaret typed away as if it were any other day and not her birthday. Katie had promised they would find some place special and affordable to eat dinner. And her mother, brother, and one or two of her sisters planned to drive in on Saturday to celebrate again. It would be a week of celebrations.

By lunchtime, both Mr. and Mrs. Corbyn were absent, so she requested a picnic meal for the park. Belgrave Square was quickly becoming one of her favorite places in London. Gretchen set the meal in motion with Cook and soon handed Margaret a basket and picnic cloth. As she crossed the street, she thanked God for the good weather. Perhaps farmers were disappointed with the dry weather they'd had through the summer, but it left her with more perfect park days than she'd anticipated since moving to London.

The birds happily tweeted their approval of the weather too as she veered off the pavement toward her favorite tree. She looked in its direction, and the spot appeared to be occupied with a couple sitting at a table and chairs—an unusual arrangement. What a disappointment. Turning, she scanned other areas of the park and tried to recall if there was another tree that might suffice for her picnic. A commotion in the direction of her tree drew her eyes back.

First she saw the waving hands, so she pointed to herself. "Me?" she whispered. She wasn't the type to yell.

A man stood while waving, and she recognized him as Mr. Corbyn. Hurrying in his direction, she noticed his mother sat beside him at the table. Awareness dawned, and she couldn't reign in her huge grin.

As she was nearly upon them, they both announced, "Happy birthday!"

"How did you know?" She wondered if Katie or her own mother had let the cat out of the bag.

Mr. Corbyn sported a sly grin, but Mrs. Corbyn spoke up. "I just love a good party, and when your mother mentioned to me that today was your birthday and she wouldn't be in until the weekend, I insisted on making the day special. Graham had the perfect suggestion to have this outside, since you've been enjoying the park so much."

Margaret scanned the table while Mrs. Corbyn spoke. It was covered with fine linens and china. "This is absolutely splendid and more than I deserve. Thank you so much for making me feel special." She wished Katie could see what they'd done for her.

"Pishposh." Mrs. Corbyn waved her hand in dismissal. "This is nothing much. Though I must admit, Cook made a mighty fine cake for you. Yet you should know, tonight will be your real birthday celebration."

"My real birthday celebration?"

"Yes, dear. Your friend Katie is coming here, and we're taking you both out for dinner." She stopped for a sip of tea. "But my lips are sealed about where we're taking you."

"Mother." Mr. Corbyn laid a hand on his mother's arm.

Mrs. Corbyn looked at him. "I said I wouldn't say more." She made the motion of zipping her lips and throwing away the key, and Mr. Corbyn shook his head.

"Please, have a seat." Mr. Corbyn stood behind a chair he pulled out for Margaret.

As Margaret sat, she noticed a lightheadedness from excitement and an ache in her cheeks from grinning so broadly.

"I hardly know what to say," Margaret admitted. "I—it's just so thoughtful, and you barely know me. And I'm only your employee."

"We know your brother and parents, and they are all . . . were all dear to me." Mr. Corbyn stumbled over the last few words. "You know what I mean."

She nodded. The loss of her father was still raw, though her bouts of sadness had lessened.

Mrs. Corbyn reached over and squeezed her hand. Her face turned somber. "Your dear brother and parents have come to mean the world to me too. They treated my son as part of their family, and I feel the same about your brother and your mother. Consider us your London family. You are much more than just an employee. I mean this sincerely."

Moisture filled Margaret's eyes, and she attempted blinking them back. One broke through, and she dabbed the corner of her eye with her napkin.

Mr. Corbyn watched her. His grave look spoke of experience. She tended to forget about his own father's passing since it had happened just before her brother met him.

"Graham, why don't you pray, and then we can share this sumptuous spread and try to turn the mood back into one of celebration." Mrs. Corbyn glanced back at Margaret. "Not that I want you to push your sadness aside, but I do want you to think of happy thoughts on your day."

"I understand. Thank you. I know you speak from experience, and I do want to be happy."

"I find that on occasions like my birthday, recalling past celebrations, when I did have my father, helps with the sadness. I also remind myself that one day, we will be together again at the best celebration— the Marriage Supper of the Lamb."

Mr. Corbyn's words lightened her heart. "Revelation." She recalled chapter nineteen, and at the same time, flashes of birthdays past with her father present spun through her mind. What joy to experience another and better celebration with him. "Thank you. That does encourage me."

Mr. Corbyn smiled and prayed, and they enjoyed the delightful garden party while Margaret's imagination danced with thoughts of the possible dinner plans the Corbyns hid.

At five p.m., the footman escorted Katie to the library as Margaret finished typing a letter. Katie wore a huge grin and squealed after the footman left.

"I've been holding this in for two days. We're going to have so much fun!"

"You know where we're going? Good job keeping it from me. It must be special if you're so excited. Care to give a hint?"

"I promised I wouldn't tell, so you'll have to wait a bit longer."

Gretchen entered and led them to one of the upstairs bedrooms, where two dresses were spread out on a mahogany canopied bed. One dress was lilac, and the other was dove gray. They had matching long gloves with them, and the dresses looked nicer than anything she owned. Both had fitted bodices and tea-length skirts that flared out from a cinched waist. She'd only seen such styles in movies.

"Are these dresses for us?" Margaret wondered out loud.

"Yes, ma'am. Mrs. Corbyn borrowed them from a friend for you. She said they're from previous seasons, so we are welcome to alter them if needed. I can do that for you." Gretchen pointed to a small basket filled with sewing items.

"Alter them?" Katie questioned as they approached the bed. "But they're perfection."

Margaret touched the lilac one. "It's dupioni silk. I saw a dress made of this when we went to Harrods."

"That's right. I remember the clerk discussing it with you," Katie said. "This one seems to be made of the same thing." Her fingers trailed down the bodice.

"I've always dreamed of wearing a dress like this." Margaret lifted the lilac dress and spun around before stopping to examine it more closely. "Hubert de Givenchy?" she read out loud from the tag. "His name sounds familiar."

"He's Audrey Hepburn's favorite dressmaker, and he's French,"

Gretchen said with a grin. "Her movies are my favorite. Have you seen *Roman Holiday*?"

Katie gasped. "Audrey Hepburn's favorite designer? I adore the clothes she wears. She's been in *Woman's Own* magazine a few times, and she's always dressed impeccably. And yes, I've seen all her movies."

"I agree about her taste in clothing. Let's get you ladies fitted."

"That dress looks lovely with your complexion." Katie touched the lilac one that Margaret held, then lifted the gray one up. "I think this pale gray one suits me best. Don't you agree?"

"I do. I believe it would wash me out, but your red hair looks striking against it."

"Wonderful," Gretchen said as she examined the dresses. "Let's see if we need to make changes. Why don't you try them on, though Mrs. Corbyn did a good job of finding someone whose clothes look nearly the right size."

"Margaret has a couple of inches in height on me, but other than that, we can usually wear the same dresses." Katie winked at her friend.

"You'll both look like princesses."

"I'm still wondering where we're going that we need to look like princesses."

"Oh, you'll see. Mrs. Corbyn does nothing by halves." Gretchen grinned as she helped Margaret into the lilac dress.

Margaret squeezed Katie's hand before they entered the reception room. Regardless of where they went, she'd never forget having the chance to go out in such style. The material felt like nothing she'd ever worn.

"You ladies look as regal as I imagined when I saw those dresses."

"Thank you so much. These are truly the most beautiful dresses I've ever seen," Margaret said.

"I agree. Thank you, ma'am."

"I'm so glad you're pleased. All eyes will be on the two of you.

Won't they, Graham?" Mrs. Corbyn nodded at her son. "I just knew Sylvia was close to the same size as you two. This makes my heart happy."

Forcing herself to glance at Mr. Corbyn, Margaret was surprised to find his eyes on her. When she smiled, color rose to his cheeks.

He cleared his throat. "Mother, would you do the honor of telling Margaret where we're going?"

Mrs. Corbyn's already smiling face lit up further. "Margaret, I'm taking you to my favorite place to celebrate birthdays and special occasions—The Ritz restaurant." She clapped her hands together.

For the second time that evening, Margaret gasped. "The Ritz restaurant?" She laid a hand over her heart and tried to catch her breath. "Oh, thank you! I never dreamed I would be able to go there. I've read articles about it and have seen a couple of pictures."

"I just love French food," Katie gushed.

"It will be a full French experience, and your French couture will be perfect." Mrs. Corbyn gestured to the front of the house. "Your chariot awaits, ladies."

Mr. Corbyn approached the women and offered each of them an arm as they exited. He helped them into the waiting car before rounding it and assisting his mother. After telling the driver goodnight, he took the driver's seat himself.

Katie chatted nearly the whole way there, but Margaret quietly watched the scenery pass as she thought about her experiences over the past week. She'd begun her day missing her mum yet excited to do something different with Katie. A smile rose to her face, and she wondered how Katie had managed to keep the secret. She'd never known her to be so tight-lipped.

Mr. Corbyn escorted them into the hotel as the valet parked their car. The Ritz was as opulent as she'd imagined. She recognized the French influence in the lobby, and the restaurant felt like a room out of a French palace, with numerous ornate gold chandeliers, cloud-filled skies painted on the sections of the ceilings and framed with gold moldings, and even mirrored walls that reminded her of her visit to Versailles.

The waiters and other workers wore black tuxedos with tails as they quietly saw to their duties around the restaurant. They seemed invisible until they were needed, then they appeared at just the right time.

Guests were dressed as elegantly as her own party and quietly conversed at their tables or greeted fellow guests as they left.

Mrs. Corbyn helped Margaret with some of the food selections she was unfamiliar with, and she was pleased with her choices. Every course was more wonderful than the previous—from the appetizers to her flaming dessert of crepes suzette. The evening was full of surprises beyond her imagination.

The night raced by, and as they left, she felt like Cinderella with the clock chiming. Their return to the Corbyns' home came all too soon.

"Thank you again for such a lovely evening," Margaret said to Mrs. Corbyn as they pulled up beside their Belgravia home. "It was like a most wonderful dream. You have truly made me feel like part of your family."

With a warm smile, Mrs. Corbyn squeezed her hand. "As it should be. It makes my heart happy to do things like this for you. See you tomorrow, dear." She turned to Katie. "And Miss O'Neil, it was a joy getting to know you better. Goodnight." With a glance at Mr. Corbyn, she added, "Get them home safely, dear."

Once Mrs. Corbyn was guided safely inside by Jones, Mr. Corbyn pulled away from the curb.

"Thank you so much for driving us home. I know it's out of your way," Katie said.

"Oh, it's nothing. Thank you, ladies, for letting my mother dote on you. Ever since she lost my sister Tracey, she's felt a gap in her life. My sister died at nine and a half years old, while Mother was pregnant with me, so I never knew her. But my parents and brother have told me what a special child she was. She'd always had heart problems, and it was like Tracey knew she wasn't long for this world. I'm told that for such a young girl, she had a heart of gold and made everyone feel special. Margaret, I think my mother sees something in you that reminds her of Tracey."

Margaret's chest constricted. "I had no idea," she choked out. "I'm so sorry your family has gone through so much. It's apparent even you have felt the loss."

"I suppose I do. I've always wondered what it would have been like to have had my older sister around growing up. I also feel the loss when I see a shadow of sadness in my mother's eyes when she's around young women. We have had our share of loss in my family. Sorry. It's a day for celebrating. Are you looking forward to seeing your mother and brother Saturday?"

"I don't mind you talking about sad things, but yes. It will be especially nice to see them both. Arthur may even bring one of my nephews or a couple of my sisters."

"You have a niece, too, don't you?"

"I do, and she's adorable, but at two, she doesn't like to leave her mum's side for long."

Mr. Corbyn chuckled. "My brother's kids are older. I miss those days."

"Margaret, what was your favorite thing about the restaurant?" Katie poked at her friend's leg.

"Do I have to choose one?"

"I'll give you some leeway since it's your birthday."

"Okay . . . hmm. I loved the way the waiters used French phrases every now and then. 'Voila! Mademoiselle. Bonne nuit.' It added to the feeling that I was in France, along with the beautiful interiors. As far as the most delicious food is concerned , it's a tie between the lobster thermidor and the mini chocolate soufflé they gave me as a birthday surprise. The soufflé was rich and light all at once, and I'd never had lobster, but that dish was also so rich, and I'll never forget it. But the most fun aspect of the meal was definitely the crepes suzette they made for me at the table. They were delicious, and the experience of watching them light my dessert on fire had me in awe."

"That was amazing to watch! I've never seen such a display at a restaurant. My favorite thing was seeing the people. I still can't believe we were seated so close to the Queen Mother. And when the French ambassador's wife stopped by to say hello to Mrs. Corbyn and we were introduced to her, I felt like royalty myself."

Both girls giggled at that.

"She even guessed the designer of our dresses." Margaret smoothed a hand over her skirt.

"They are French designers, after all. We looked like princesses in them. Don't you think, Mr. Corbyn?"

"Yes, of course." He pointed to Ealing Common. "We're nearly to your place."

"We are," Katie said.

"Do you think you might try to move somewhere closer to your jobs since you both work in my direction?" he asked.

Margaret looked at Katie, who raised an eyebrow. "The area where you live is expensive. We had to go out this far to find somewhere safe and reasonable."

"Unless you want to give Margaret a big raise, of course," Katie said.

Margaret's eyes went wide, and she gave Katie a pointed look.

"Would you move closer if you could afford it?" Mr. Corbyn asked.

"Of course we would." Katie spoke for them both.

"If it were a decent place and safe, yes," Margaret added.

"Okay." Mr. Corbyn nodded but stared past her at Mrs. Fletcher's boarding home as he pulled up next to the curb.

He hopped out of the car and helped both ladies out, then escorted them to the front door. "Goodnight, Katie." He tipped his hat to her before turning to Margaret. "Goodnight, Margaret." Lifting her gloved hand, he added, "And happiest of birthdays to you. I'll see you tomorrow."

There was that familiar tingle again. She had to shut it down, but the more she knew of him, the more handsome she found him. "Yes. See you then and thank you for making this whole day special." Recalling their lunch in the park, her heart fluttered. His mother may have planned it, but he was the one who told her how much Margaret enjoyed the park and specifically that tree.

"I'm honored to be part of it." He dipped his head and dropped her hand. "Tomorrow," he said before walking away.

As he opened the car door, he turned and glanced their way once more, and Margaret sighed softly.

"I knew it," Katie said as they entered the house. "You still like him as more than a friend."

"I can't exactly turn off my feelings, though I am trying."

"I'm only teasing. I don't blame you and am still rooting for the two of you to end up together. He doesn't have a ring on his finger yet."

"I'd prefer not to get my hopes up. Maybe when I see him with Miss Fairfax, I'll have a better idea of the story with the two of them."

Katie tapped her chin as they walked up the stairs. "Yes, I am curious about Miss Frances Fairfax."

Chapter Seven

Miss Frances Fairfax was beautiful in all the ways society measured beauty. Her average height complemented her hourglass figure and shiny, perfectly coiffed chestnut hair. Her familiarity with the butler was apparent when he sent her directly to the office without announcing her arrival.

"I've come to make sure you're working, Graham," Miss Fairfax called out from the open library door.

"Busy as ever, but I can take a break for you."

"Excellent, darling." Miss Fairfax turned to Margaret. "And you must be Miss Margaret Elliot. It's so good to finally meet you in person. It will be nice to have another woman around. May I call you Margaret?"

"Of course, Miss Fairfax."

"You may call me Frances, dear." She flashed her left hand at Margaret, showing off a large diamond engagement ring. "We'll be seeing each other often, and I'm sure we'll become fast friends."

Margaret's smile wobbled. "Certainly . . . Frances. It's good to meet you too."

Frances smiled and walked over to Graham, who stood in greeting. She air-kissed him on both cheeks before settling down in the chair in front of him and laying a tied-up pile of paper on the desk.

Margaret tried to focus on the work in front of her yet couldn't help but listen to their conversation and attempt to read between the lines of what they said.

"The manuscript was good. I recommend publishing the book."

"Perfect." Mr. Corbyn picked up the bundle and laid it on a pile to his right. "I'll have my solicitor draw up a contract and contact the author's agent."

Frances nodded. "Do you have us booked for lunch, dear? I figured we could discuss things over lunch. I have to meet the wedding planner at two."

"Can we eat here today? It will give you a chance to get to know Margaret."

"I'm sure I can make that work."

"How was Cannes?" Mr. Corbyn asked.

"Hot. Mother insisted we stay for the full two weeks, and I'm glad to be back. It was nice at first, but I missed everyone here."

"I would say it was quiet around here without you, but as you can see"—he waved toward Margaret—"things have been busy."

Frances smiled at Margaret. "I do see." She tapped the desk with her fingers. "So what's next? Do you have another manuscript for me to read over?"

"I do and am glad to have you back to help." Mr. Corbyn reached into one of his drawers and pulled out a large envelope. "I hope you can read it quickly. It seems someone is poaching some of the authors we've been courting."

"Well, that is disconcerting," Frances said with a tilt of her head and raised brow. She looked at her watch. "I think a good meal might help us deal with such a blow. Do you think Cook has lunch ready?"

Mr. Corbyn checked his watch too. "I'll ring for Miss Hoffman. I'd say it's close enough to ready. Are you hungry, Miss Elliot?"

Margaret fought not to let on that she'd been eavesdropping. "Oh. Yes, I can eat now. I'm just finishing up something."

"Wonderful. I think the two of you will get along smashingly."

In the dining room, Mr. Corbyn sat at the head of the table with Frances on his right and Margaret on his left. Throughout lunch, Margaret analyzed the interactions and words spoken between Mr.

Corbyn and Frances. She was determined to know if Mr. Corbyn was Frances's fiancé. By the end of lunch, she'd still not decided. They acted very familiar with each other, but she couldn't categorize their looks, conversations, and periodic touches as either more friendly or more romantic. It was quite a letdown.

She did learn they'd grown up together with their families closeknit, and Frances's parents' home, where she currently lived, was only a block away.

"I hate to eat and run," Frances said, "but I do have that appointment, and I need to stop by my house first."

"What will you be discussing with the wedding planner?"

"Food for the reception."

"Make sure to have things I like."

Frances chuckled. "Yes, I know all the foods you like and will be sure to have plenty there you'll eat." She looked at Margaret and winked. "Men. It seems the way to their hearts truly is food. On that note, I really have to run. It was so good to meet you, Margaret. We'll have to go out sometime without Graham." She winked and turned to Mr. Corbyn. "Graham, walk me out, please."

Mr. Corbyn left the dining room with Frances and returned several minutes later—with mussed hair and pink cheeks. He looked at Margaret, and the color in his cheeks rose. "I think I'll get back to work. You're welcome to stay and enjoy the rest of your break or go for a walk in the park to finish your lunch break."

"Thanks. I . . . I think I'll get back to work too."

That evening in their room, Margaret rehashed Mr. Corbyn and Frances's interactions with Katie and determined she was no closer to defining their relationship. "I've decided it doesn't matter. I shouldn't be pining after my much older boss who is also my brother's good friend. I never should have let myself get carried away. I don't know what I was thinking."

"You were hoping he would be different than John."

Margaret nodded, but the reminder stung.

"But you were so young then, and he was immature. Everyone knows that boys take longer to mature. That's one reason Mr. Corbyn might be perfect for you."

"Thanks, but I'm really giving up on Mr. Corbyn this time. Instead, I want to focus my efforts on figuring out ways to help the company. I overheard Mr. Corbyn talking to Frances and telling her he thinks someone is poaching authors our company is pursuing. I plan to help him figure out how to get them to choose to stay with us."

"Ooh. I like the sound of this. So you were spying, and you want to plan more undercover shenanigans to get authors to choose your company." She clapped her hands together and rubbed them.

"What? There's no spying or shenanigans. I accidentally overheard them. It's hard not to when he's in the same room as me."

"Yes, and you can use that to your advantage to get him to look at you as more than an employee."

"Katie, be serious. I already told you, I've seen the error of my ways."

"But he's the man you're going to marry one day. You said that."

"It must have been delirium. I'm better now. So . . . back to what I was saying. There's this situation, and I have some ideas that I want to talk through with you. Tell me if they sound a bit dotty."

Katie stretched out on the bed tummy down and tucked her hands under her chin. "Oh, I can tell you right now, you're barking mad. But that has more to do with you choosing to not pursue the man who is perfect for you. Aside from that, I'll try to help you with this other situation."

"May I have a few minutes of your time to discuss an idea?" Margaret asked Mr. Corbyn the next morning after Mrs. Corbyn left the dining room. Though she liked her ideas, she wondered if he would appreciate them.

"Of course. You seemed distracted during the Bible study." He furrowed his brow. "Is something bothering you?"

She shook her head. "I'm sorry. I did try to focus on the study, and I managed to get something out of it."

The furrow disappeared. "Let's hear it." He guided her into a lounge chair in the library, maintaining the open door as promised.

Words she'd fought to hold back during the Bible study seemed to have fled, and she searched for how to begin while staring at her folded hands. "I . . ." She looked up and caught him watching her with a tender smile that made her heart leap and jumbled her thoughts more.

Shifting her gaze down again, the haze cleared. "What if we made packets for the authors you are pursuing to help them feel like they are part of something special—which of course they are." As she spoke, she relaxed, and the words began to flow. "The packets could contain items like a prayer and Bible study journal we design with our name and verses throughout." Hazarding a glance upward, she found his smile had grown, revealing dimples in both cheeks. It set off all of the features that had drawn her to him the first day, but she quickly determined not to let it sidetrack her and pushed forward explaining her plan. "We could choose a theme verse for our company, and that could be a key verse used on the outside of the journal and on a specially crafted bookmark. We could also add it to letterheads, business cards, and advertisements."

"Margaret, your idea is brilliant. Yes to all of it. You are amazing."

"I have more ideas too. We could invite the authors to our morning Bible studies so they feel even more a part of things and can get to know the heart of our company. I even have ideas about the bookmarks. My mum is part of a women's group that does sewing crafts to raise money for missions projects. We could commission them to make bookmarks for the female authors. For the men, we could have them constructed from leather. I know an honest leather craftsman back home we could hire." She paused for a breath.

"Incredible." He crossed a leg and tapped his chin. "You heard my conversation with Frances yesterday?"

"I did. I'm sorry."

He chuckled. "If a conversation needs to be private, I'll leave. It's not your fault.

And I hope you won't worry. We'll get through this. But I do think your ideas will make a huge difference. Feel free to share any other ideas you have."

"Thank you. I'll admit I was a little worried when I heard you tell Frances about the authors. I like my job, and I'd like to keep it."

"We're a new publishing house, so it's going to take an extra effort to give authors confidence. Please don't worry though—I have the funds to keep us going. I've also been praying about it, too, and now that we're talking about it, I would very much appreciate you praying as well. Perhaps it will take creativity like yours to help people see we are worth the risk."

"I keep a list of Bible verses I love and can use them on the pages of the journal if you'd like."

"Thank you. What a treasure those journals will be."

"I've also been thinking about our theme verse."

"It's funny you brought that up. Even before this conversation, I'd decided we needed a verse. I'd thought about it before you came, but since we started the Romans study, God has brought it to the forefront of my mind."

"He keeps bringing it to mine too." She thought of the verse God had placed on her heart the night before, Romans 15:13. "God was pointing me to a verse on hope."

Mr. Corbyn's eyes grew wide, and his smile brightened. "Romans 15:13. May the God of hope fill you with all joy and peace in believing, so that by the power of the Holy Spirit, you may abound in hope. Is that the one you were thinking of?"

Margaret's heart felt like it skipped a beat. "It is. That's the verse God directed me to. How did you know?"

"He directed me to the same verse, and I've been memorizing it."

"That's . . ." She shook her head, trying to grasp what she'd learned.

"Remarkable?" He finished her sentence. "Our God is remarkable. We make an excellent team, Miss Elliot, and it seems we've got our work cut out for us. Let's set these things in motion."

"I've already started a list." She handed him the notepad she'd tucked beside her leg in the chair.

"You continue to astonish me. Keep this up, and I'll be helpless without you."

"I do hope to give you reasons to keep me around." The moment she said it, she regretted her words. Try as she would, both meanings held true. "I'll . . . um . . . I think there's something I need to type. After you look that over, I'll be happy to type it up for you." Heat rose to her cheeks as she moved to her desk.

"Miss Elliot, I do appreciate it. If you're willing, I'd like to delegate tasks between us after looking over the list. If I consider changing anything, I'll discuss it with you first, though at first glance, it looks perfect." He moved to his own desk. "All these years, I thought God had placed your brother and me together just so I could have a good friend through life's ups and downs. Yet it seems God's plan was bigger than I imagined."

A mixture of joy and awe filled Margaret as she began typing. She soon forgot her initial embarrassment. *God truly is remarkable.*

Chapter Eight

Philippians 1:21-24. *For to me to live is Christ, and to die is gain. If it is to be life in the flesh, that means fruitful labor for me. Yet which I shall choose I cannot tell. I am hard pressed between the two. My desire is to depart and be with Christ, for that is far better. But to remain in the flesh is more necessary on your account.*

Standing with Katie on the portico of the Corbyns' home, waiting for someone to answer her knock, Margaret mulled over the verses she'd written in her journal on the bus ride over. Though she looked forward to seeing her mother and brother, working on verses for the publishing journal had become nearly all-consuming.

Jones greeted Margaret and Katie at the door and escorted them into the parlor, where she found her mother and brother chatting with Mr. Corbyn and his mother.

Looking up and seeing Margaret, her mother beamed, and she rushed to meet her with an embrace. "Margaret. I know it's only been a week, but it seems so much longer since I left, and it's the first time I've missed celebrating your birthday with you."

"It was a bit strange, but I'm happy to see you now, Mum. I've been looking forward to today."

"Meg." Her brother Arthur approached and gave her a side hug.

"How's this chap treating you?" He pointed to Mr. Corbyn, who raised a brow.

"Quite well."

"She's become indispensable to me, and I'm doing everything I can to make sure she stays," Mr. Corbyn stated.

Margaret's cheeks heated at all the attention.

Arthur crossed his arms. "Indispensable? And what *are* you doing to make sure she stays?"

Mr. Corbyn glanced at his mum, and she nodded. "Miss Elliot, Mother and I wanted to offer you and Katie the mews house to live in. It would alleviate all of the buses the two of you have to take for work and will save you both money and time."

"The mews house behind yours . . . where you keep your cars?" Margaret found the offer hard to believe.

"Yes, there are three bedrooms in the apartment attached to it."

"Three bedrooms?" Katie parroted.

Mr. Corbyn nodded.

"And where will you move, Graham?" Arthur asked.

Margaret's eyes flew to Mr. Corbyn's as the implication hit. "You live in the mews house?"

"I'll move into this home with Mother."

"There's so much room, I'll hardly even know he's here," Mrs. Corbyn chimed in.

"Mr. Corbyn, I won't take your home." Margaret couldn't imagine a man of his age wanting to move in with his mum.

"You wouldn't be taking it. I would be giving it to you. I want to do this. It's no hardship for me."

"But . . . it doesn't make sense," Margaret admitted.

"Why don't we go to the morning room for tea? We can talk about it more there." Mrs. Corbyn stood and led the way.

Margaret turned to follow and hoped she could make them understand her concerns without seeming rude, but a tug at her elbow stopped her. It was Mr. Corbyn.

"I hope you'll seriously consider the offer. You don't have to decide today, but it would mean a lot to me if you accepted."

She bit her lip and wondered how best to answer. Her mind shuffled through the pros and cons for herself, Katie, and the Corbyns. "We can't afford to pay you what it is worth. If you move, you should at least get what the home is worth. You can rent it to someone who can afford it."

"It's not ever been rented out, and Mother doesn't need the money. In my lifetime, it has only been used by our family driver or actual family. My brother is married and has his own home, and I would prefer the two of you live in it than have to traverse through half of London every morning and night for work. I've lived with my mother before as an adult, and we got along quite well. But like she said, the house is big enough that we would hardly cross paths except for meals, and we eat together anyway. All that to say, you can live there rent-free, and it would not be a burden to me or Mother. Quite the opposite. It would please us both."

"Mr. Corbyn, I—"

"Please think it over."

"I suppose I can do that." She smiled at him, hoping it conveyed her appreciation for his thoughtfulness. As she looked into his eyes, awareness filled her—of his nearness and of his lingering touch on her elbow. Her heart leaped, and she quickly stepped back, recalling the promise to herself and also his possible engagement.

In the morning room, Mr. Corbyn led her to the sideboard where a silver tea set, porcelain teacups with saucers, and a tiered stand filled with finger sandwiches, small cakes, and tartlets awaited them.

"May I pour you some tea?" Mr. Corbyn asked Margaret.

"Yes. Thank you." She looked over the labels in front of each tea. "I'll take the—"

"Darjeeling?"

A chuckle broke free from her throat. "Yes. I suppose you would know what I drink by now."

"I do. You're welcome to try something different, but I've noticed you're a creature of habit when it comes to tea."

"Oh, really?" His comment felt like a challenge. "And how do I take my Darjeeling?"

"With one sugar cube." He reached for the sugar tong.

Margaret bit back her smile but hesitated to answer. "Okay, you *have* been paying attention. Thank you. May I serve you some sandwiches or cake?"

"Thank you, I'll take two of each of the sandwiches and a cake and tartlet."

"Of course. They all look so good." She put together a plate for him and one for herself while he poured their tea. She kept an eye on him to see if he would pour himself Earl Grey with no sugar or cream, and silently praised herself for her own attentiveness when he did.

Once they had their food, she found Katie had saved her a seat on a sofa opposite from a matching one where her brother sat awaiting Mr. Corbyn. Their mothers sat in Queen Anne chairs placed together at one end of the sofas.

"Margaret, we would have liked to have sent a car for you and Katie," Mrs. Corbyn said.

Margaret set her tea down on the coffee table. "The bus was no trouble."

Katie spoke up. "I think Margaret preferred having the extra time to work on verses for that journal she's doing for Mr. Corbyn."

His eyes found Margaret's, and his brow furrowed. "You don't need to be working on your days off."

"I don't think of it as work but as doing a Bible study. And I've been so excited about working on the journal that ideas of things to add are constantly popping into my mind. I bring the journal and my small Bible everywhere with me, just in case I have an inspiration."

"Tell me more, dear, about what you're working on," her mother said. "Graham mentioned a packet for authors and a theme verse for the company. He said God gave you both the same verse."

That familiar burning flame of excitement filled Margaret as she recalled the realization they'd had. "God did. He gave us both the same verse, which confirmed it was what God had planned." She looked at Graham, who nodded her onward, so she explained how she was using verses from her own journal and adding to them to create a journal for the authors to use for their own Bible study and prayer times. As she spoke, Mr. Corbyn encouraged her with nods and smiles.

"Your father would be so proud. He worked all of his adult life to share God's Word, and here you are following in his footsteps in your own way. And what a lovely gift that will be for the authors," Mrs. Elliot praised her daughter.

"I couldn't agree more," Mr. Corbyn cut in. "All of the ideas for the journal and gift basket were Miss Elliot's. Arthur, I'm more thankful than you can imagine that you recommended your sister. She couldn't be more perfect for me. Her creativity is beyond compare, and her faith carries over into everything she does."

Mr. Corbyn's smiles and compliments made Margaret's heart flutter despite her determination against those feelings, and she silently prayed God would help her keep her mind and heart in check and for her actions to follow suit.

"My sister may be quiet, but she loves the Lord and shares his love with others. She also does everything she sets her mind to with excellence. I'm not surprised that you've quickly discovered those qualities, especially since your company actively pursues the same things that drive her."

Mr. Corbyn nodded and continued with his praise of her. "As I've said, Miss Elliot has brought much clarity and creativity to our new company, and I already cannot imagine the place without her. Let's all raise our cups to Miss Elliot." As Mr. Corbyn lifted his teacup, heat rose to Margaret's face. But he continued. "To good ideas and good people— may we keep hold of both."

She smiled at him when she realized he also meant that she was helping him keep hold of the authors they pursued. Her mother and brother both seemed pleased with the toast and joined with their hearty affirmation.

"Have you decided on a plan for the day, Mum?" Arthur asked.

"After talking things through with Lavinia"—she nodded at Mrs. Corbyn—"I think we should visit the exhibition of the Royal Academy. I've not laid eyes on the portrait of the Queen by Annigoni that everyone is talking about. We could then walk through Green Park past Buckingham Palace, then take a taxi to the Strand for lunch. I'll likely need a break after that. This evening, the Corbyns are hosting us for dinner, and they've reserved tickets for *Sailor Beware!* at the Strand Theatre."

She turned to Mrs. Corbyn. "I do appreciate how you've taken Margaret and Katie under your wing. The way you spoiled them on Margaret's birthday and today means so much."

"Pishposh." She waved her hand. "Like I told them, it's nothing. But truly, I can imagine how lost I'd feel in their situation, and I'm glad I could do something special for them. But I can't take all of the credit. Graham made sure I treated Margaret right on her birthday, and I do enjoy having young ladies around to spoil. In fact"—Mrs. Corbyn turned to Margaret and Katie—"Sylvia came through again for the two of you, and I have the most lovely dresses waiting upstairs for you to wear to the theatre."

"Thank you," the two said nearly in unison.

Margaret couldn't imagine anything as lovely as the dresses they wore to her birthday dinner, but after seeing the good taste of Mrs. Corbyn's friend, she trusted her completely and looked forward to wearing one of the dresses to the theatre. She'd always enjoyed occasions to dress up, but having two in one week would be a treat.

Margaret shifted in her seat as the intermission began and was reminded of her overfull tummy from dinner at the Corbyns'. They'd had seven courses, and each one was exquisite—from the appetizer of potted shrimps to the trifle of mixed berries and custard. After so many years of rationing, such delicacies felt especially extravagant. The family had made her feel extra special this week. She'd even met Mr. Corbyn's brother and sister-in-law, who joined them for dinner before they left for the theatre.

Margaret looked around the elegant theatre, with its gilded decorative molding, intricate ceiling decorations, and velvet-covered seats. Everyone else in her party except herself and Mr. Corbyn had stepped away from the Corbyns' box. She scanned the crowd as they milled around. The patrons were dressed in their best, including Margaret and Katie. This time, Margaret's dress was a full-length ivory gown with a sweetheart neckline and off-the-shoulder sleeves accentuating her figure. Katie's was emerald green, highlighting her eyes and hair perfectly. With the pearls Mrs. Corbyn loaned them, they were elegant enough to meet the Queen.

They were, in fact, in the presence of royalty. Mr. Corbyn informed her that the Queen's sister, Margaret, was in attendance and sat in the royal box on the opposite side of the theatre. She lifted her opera glasses to see more clearly, and there sat Princess Margaret, elegantly dressed in a pastel floral dress with a dramatic V-neck. It was the second time in one week she'd seen royalty.

"Would you like me to order you something to drink? They have tea as well as other things," Mr. Corbyn asked Margaret.

"Oh, no, I can't put another thing into my mouth. I overdid it during dinner. I enjoyed it all, but if Cook keeps feeding me like that, I won't fit through the door."

Mr. Corbyn chuckled. "It's been a while since Mother entertained with an elegant dinner like that, and Cook was eager to make some of her special dishes. But if you don't care for that kind of food, I'll see to it she doesn't do that again for you."

"Oh, no. I'll work on pacing myself. It really was delicious."

A tap on her shoulder drew her attention, and she looked back to see Frances had stopped by their box.

"Hello, darling. Isn't this show perfectly absurd? I don't think I've laughed like this in ages."

Margaret was surprised Frances spoke to her when Mr. Corbyn sat only two seats away. Yet Frances looked directly at her. "It is terribly clever. I had no idea you'd be here tonight. Mr. Corbyn never mentioned it."

Frances waved a hand in the air. "I like to keep him guessing. But truly, I came by to introduce you to my fiancé." She looked back and pulled a handsome dark-haired man forward. "Margaret, I'd like you to meet William Ainsworth, my fiancé. William, this is my new friend and coworker, Margaret Elliot."

A strange feeling came over Margaret—a mixture of relief and giddiness.

Mr. Corbyn stood and offered Margaret a hand to join him.

She accepted it, and he helped her to her feet. Could he feel her tremble as she contained her emotions and tried to make sense of them?

"Pleased to meet you, Miss Elliot." Mr. Ainsworth inclined his head.

"It's very nice to meet you, Mr. Ainsworth." Margaret gave a polite nod.

"Frances told me about you," he said. "I'm glad to hear Graham has someone there to keep him in line."

Margaret's face heated, and she gathered her wits to say, "I do what I can to help things run smoothly." She couldn't bring herself to make Mr. Corbyn out to be a difficult employer.

"She's just being modest, Will. I don't know what I'd do without her. She may not realize it, but in the short time she's been there, I've come to rely on her guidance in nearly all of my marketing and author relations. Our skills complement one another's well."

"I'll say." Mr. Ainsworth raised a brow and glanced between the two of them. "Sounds like a match made in heaven."

Margaret was at a loss for words. He surely didn't mean for that to sound the way it did, but it had her mind retreading places it shouldn't —namely, marriage.

"Right you are." Mr. Corbyn chuckled softly.

Frances interjected. "I spoke with your mother in the lobby, Graham. Seems we missed a delightful dinner." She turned to Margaret. "William's parents are in town, and we'd committed to eat with them, or I would have joined."

"I understand." She folded her gloved hands in front of her, attempting to keep from fidgeting as her mind worked to keep up with the conversation. She couldn't stop ruminating over the idea that Graham was not engaged.

The others began returning to their seats, and Frances and Mr. Ainsworth greeted them before saying their goodbyes.

During the second half of the play, Margaret struggled to follow the plot with her mind continuing to wander towards the man sitting two seats down. The news that he wasn't engaged shouldn't have changed how she felt. She'd promised herself she would focus on her writing and work at the company and told herself he wasn't appropriate for her. But her heart insisted she reevaluate those decisions.

As the curtain closed, she was still undecided about whether her heart or mind would win the battle over Mr. Corbyn.

Chapter Nine

Staying at the Corbyns' home Saturday night and going to church and lunch with them on Sunday swung the pendulum in the direction of Margaret's heart. By the time her mother and brother left, she was well on her way to ignoring her mind. Their words and actions didn't help. They appeared rather pleased every time Mr. Corbyn and Margaret ended up sitting together or in conversation. And they were quite happy when she and Katie accepted the invitation to move into the Corbyns' mews home.

They had promised to give Mrs. Fletcher a one-week notice before moving out of her boardinghouse, and Mr. Corbyn said that was more than enough time for him to move his things. The furniture was to stay in the home, so it would make an easy transition for them too.

By Monday, Margaret was ready for the week to be over. Nervous energy filled her, and she worked to focus it on her tasks. When lunchtime finally came, she needed fresh air in her favorite spot in the park. Mr. Corbyn had left soon after she'd shown up that morning, so she requested a picnic basket and rushed out as soon as it arrived.

The birds were chirping, and the air felt cooler than it had earlier in the week. If she were back home under her willow tree, she would take off her shoes and walk through the grass barefoot. She chuckled at the thought of being caught barefoot in Belgrave Square.

Setting her basket aside, she stretched out the quilt and leaned up against the tree with her Bible, inhaling the fresh air. Her mind might be distracted, but she longed for the refreshment of God's Word more than thoughts of Graham Corbyn.

She flipped to Matthew 6, knowing exactly what passage would help her. She scanned down to verse twenty-five. *Therefore I tell you, do not be anxious about your life, what you shall eat or what you shall drink, nor about your body, what you shall put on. Is not life more than food, and the body more than clothing? Look at the birds of the air: they neither sow nor reap nor gather into barns, and yet your Heavenly Father feeds them. Are you not of more value than they?* Her eyes caught on a bird just landing on a branch in the tree nearest hers. *Yes, God, I hear you.*

Finding her place again, she continued reading about the lilies of the field and slowed when she read the last two verses of the passage. *But seek first his kingdom and his righteousness, and all these things shall be yours as well. Therefore do not be anxious about tomorrow, for tomorrow will be anxious for itself. Let the day's own trouble be sufficient for the day.*

She closed the Bible and her eyes. *God, you are so good and trustworthy. Help me follow you and not worry.* She paused. "Trust me," echoed in her mind. *I do, Lord.* "Trust me." *I think I am trusting you.* "Trust me." *Okay.*

When she opened her eyes, there Mr. Corbyn stood, only a few feet away, looking at the very tree she had seen the bird land in. She took in his silhouette before the urge to stop herself from admiring him overcame her. Yet the very scripture she'd been studying came to mind. She'd been working herself up all weekend about the outcome of considering a relationship with Mr. Corbyn. Maybe it would be better if instead of ruling out a relationship with him, she let things unfold naturally—the way God intended. She wouldn't force it either. If it was God's plan, he would need to make it abundantly clear.

Margaret cleared her throat, and Mr. Corbyn turned to her.

"I apologize. I could see you were praying and didn't want to interrupt, so I turned away. Do you mind if I join you?"

"Of course not."

He raised a hand holding a sack. "I picked up a sandwich and lemonade and hurried home to join you. I had a feeling you'd be eating out on this nice day, but I forgot to ask Cook to make me a picnic lunch."

She smiled at him and felt at peace. Was this how God was working? When he pulled out his wax paper-covered sandwich, she caught a whiff of mustard.

"Smells tasty."

"I've eaten at the café before and always enjoyed their ham and mustard. Would you like half? It's already cut."

"Oh, no. I won't eat your sandwich. But you are welcome to have some of my coronation chicken salad. Cook always gives me more than I can eat. And after this weekend, I need to eat a bit less."

"I don't think you need to worry about what you ate this weekend. You're doing just fine. Cook does make a good coronation chicken salad though."

Margaret lifted the glass container filled with the salad from her basket. "See? There's plenty." She knew Cook always included an extra plate and utensils, and it seemed a waste until now as she spooned out a scoop of the salad. "Here. You can have this. There's another plate for me." She held up the second plate.

"So when did you decide you wanted to come to London and work for a publishing company?" Mr. Corbyn asked after Margaret swallowed her last bite of the tasty ham sandwich she'd taken after his insistence.

Tightness encircled Margaret. It sounded like a simple question, but it was tied to events she'd tried to forget. Ones that exposed her weaknesses. *Do not be anxious. Trust me.* She took a deep breath. "I used to think . . ." Her voice trailed off. Could she do this? Should she tell him? She closed her eyes, then opened them to find him patiently waiting.

"I used to think I would get married at a young age, have babies, and write as a hobby. I hoped to publish someday but had no timeline. But then, well—" How to say this? "The reason I thought I would get married young is because I thought I was in love at fourteen. His name was John Sinclair." She looked into his eyes, expecting censure, but found none, yet her gaze drifted to her hands.

"He was sixteen and promised we would get married after he did his time in the army. Instead, his parents sent him away for his A-levels at seventeen, and then he started university at Cambridge. I rarely saw him, and the letters became fewer and further apart. It wasn't until Christmas vacation that he admitted his parents had found out about us only a few months after we started seeing each other, and they'd sent him away for A-levels because of me. They said he was intended for a wealthy heiress." She looked up from her hands to check his reaction. "Did I mention he was to inherit an earldom?"

Mr. Corbyn shook his head, a frown marring his handsome face.

"He was, and he told me that his parents also said a wife who writes fantastical stories not only couldn't be trusted to raise children properly but would reflect poorly on his family. They called my stories 'flights of fancy' and said they could never take me seriously. He didn't stand up to them. I think he secretly agreed. They told him that if I wanted to be an author, I should remain single as Miss Austen did."

Mr. Corbyn furrowed his brow. "And you took their advice?"

"It does seem to fit. It's ironic, isn't it? Jane Austen was from the very same town as me, her father was a pastor like mine, and something similar happened to her. Of course, with modern medicine, I don't think my life will end so early, and my sister closest in age was recently married. I do have Katie . . . though I doubt she'll be single much longer. She desperately wants to get married."

He leaned in. "You don't?"

She took a deep breath. "I . . . told myself I didn't."

"Past tense?"

She shrugged. She wasn't sure anymore. "I don't know. Anyway, what was it you asked me in the first place?" The current topic made her increasingly uncomfortable.

"I asked when you decided to come to London and work for a publishing company."

She nodded as she remembered. "I decided since I wasn't going to get married, I should get a job to support myself so I could write and publish my books. A publishing company seemed to make the most sense."

It was hard to maintain eye contact as she bared her soul, so her eyes found the trees behind him. "When my father died, it became even more important that I support myself. My mum decided to move in with Arthur and his family, and I knew time was running out. They didn't need another person to house with their growing family. Katie and I had already talked about London, and since she wasn't seeing anyone back home, we planned to come here together. We'd talked about it off and on for ages."

Looking up, she found him watching her closely. "You're doubting whether I'm right for your company and wondering how a woman with flights of fancy like I have can do anything worthwhile to retain your authors."

He shook his head slowly. "I'm wondering how that idiot believed any of that drivel when the woman in front of me is nothing like that. I'm thinking he missed his opportunity with you, and you will make someone the happiest man alive."

She could hardly believe her ears. Surely he wasn't serious. He didn't know her well enough to see where she was lacking. "I heard John is engaged now." That had been another hard hit that reaffirmed her choice to remain single.

"Unless she's exactly like you, he'll regret it the rest of his life." The corner of his mouth curled up.

She couldn't hold back her own smile and shook her head. "Thank you. For believing in me and encouraging me. I try not to get stuck in my feelings and don't like to tell my story, because I don't want others to feel sorry for me."

"Oh, I don't feel sorry for you." He chuckled softly. "Once you shake off the remnants of what that John bloke told you, you're going to take the publishing world by storm—both as an author and running the show at our publishing company."

"Running the show? Our company?"

"It may be my name on the letterhead, but I foresee you having a huge impact on everything the company does."

"Mr. Corbyn, you can't be serious."

"You've been locked in a box that John and his parents put you in, but I've seen you pushing to break out of it. I'm glad you feel comfortable enough to spread your wings around me." He tapped his chin. "In fact, it's time you called me by my first name. You've earned it."

"But Mr. Corbyn—"

"Graham."

"I don't understand."

"Neither do I. I just know that in the past two weeks you've turned my world upside down. I thought I had all of the answers, but you came, and now I can't do without you."

The intensity between them was too much, and she broke eye contact. Surely he only referred to work he couldn't do without her. She took a deep breath to slow her racing heart.

"I . . . thank you." She wasn't sure what the appropriate response was and felt awkward after their conversation. "I have some things to type. And if I'm that indispensable to you, I should probably make sure you get busy too."

He chuckled and nodded as he loaded things into the basket, then helped her up. They were both silent as they walked back to the house. Something had shifted between them.

When they stood in front of the door, she turned to him and tried out his name. "Graham, you can call me Margaret."

"Thank you . . . Margaret. How about when others are around during the workday, we use Mr. and Miss, but after hours and in private, we use first names?"

Butterflies filled her chest as he reached around her to open the door.

"Yes, that's probably best."

Chapter Ten

Three weeks had passed since Margaret and Graham had their heart-to-heart. She and Katie were settled in the mews house, and Graham and Mrs. Corbyn were a constant in her life.

She and Graham had just left the new office after meeting the interior decorator to go over some of the final decisions. Tomorrow they would work in their new office as the decorator brought in the last of the furniture and accessories.

It was a beautiful space with a combination of modern and traditional furniture and accessories. The ambiance gave a sense of promise for the future without being ostentatious. Soothing sage and cream with a touch of navy made it both relaxing and professional. She had her own desk in the reception area, where floor-to-ceiling bookcases lined one wall. Another wall was accented with an elegant antique bookcase Graham said he purchased soon after deciding to open his own publishing house.

Having a space of her own might relieve the anxiety she felt every time they were alone. Regardless of where their offices were physically located, the amount of work they did together and their shared meals at the Belgravia home kept them together much of the day and added to the tension. She'd accepted that God might be doing something between them, but she wasn't going to force anything to happen. If it was God's plan, he would have to make it abundantly clear.

Currently, Graham sat before her, sipping mineral water from a bottle at Wellington Grill. It was a pleasant restaurant in a converted townhouse across from the Corbyn office building, where the publishing company was located.

"What looks good to you today, Margaret?"

"Mmm. I just might try their grilled plaice with caper butter."

"I saw a waiter walk by carrying that, and it looked delicious. I'm getting the lamb chop with minted peas and new potatoes. Yours comes with two sides also."

"I'll get the cucumber tomato salad and the new potatoes too." Pleased with her choices, she closed the menu.

He nodded to their waiter, who came and took their order.

Once they were alone again, he grinned. "Let's see the copy of our Bible journal by our very own Miss Margaret Elliot."

Margaret grinned as she pulled it out of her bag. They'd approved a proof copy two days earlier, and this copy was from the first run. "I love the way it turned out." She flipped through the book after looking again at the cover. "It may not be one of my fiction books, but I still can't believe I have something published."

Mr. Corbyn reached for it with a broad smile. "I can. You're an amazing author of both fiction and"—he held up the journal—"nonfiction."

"Thank you," she said softly and looked away. He didn't seem real. After the way John had discarded her, she doubted a man would ever look at her and say such things about her writing unless it had been thoroughly edited, polished, and packaged so it was barely recognizable. She'd hoped her work could one day stand on its own, but Frances had looked the journal over and declared it nearly perfect. Graham even let Margaret work with the cover designer to give her input. The final product was hardly changed from her original plan.

She felt his hand lightly touch hers. "Margaret, I'm being sincere, and I'll say it as many times as necessary until you believe it—you are amazing. I've never met anyone like you. You excel in creativity and logic, and you do it all with excellence. You are absolutely brilliant."

He squeezed her hand before pulling it back. Her heart fluttered. Was he interested in her as more than his secretary? Were feelings growing inside of him the way they were in her?

She watched as his eyes followed a middle-aged woman nearing their table. The woman glanced at him, then quickly looked away with a furrow in her brow.

"Mrs. Brown, how are you?" he said as she passed the table. "Mrs. Brown?"

She stopped and turned to him. She pursed her lips before saying, "Quite well, Mr. Corbyn."

"I'd like you to meet my assistant, Miss Elliot. She is the one who sent you the last letter. Miss Elliot, this is Mrs. Brown, one of the authors who considered working with us."

"So good to meet you, Mrs. Brown. I just happen to have something for you." She lifted the Bible journal that was lying on Graham's side of the table and handed it to Mrs. Brown. "This is from the first run of Bible journals we designed and printed especially for the authors we are considering working with, so they can see the quality of work our company does and also know that we truly are committed to helping them draw closer to God. This one was specifically designed with authors in mind. It has our theme verse right here at the beginning." Margaret opened the book and pointed to the verse, then flipped through it so Mrs. Brown could see the layout.

"Why . . ." She glanced at Graham before looking back at Margaret. "Thank you. But that's unnecessary since I've . . . well, you know." Her eyes shifted to the floor.

"Oh, we insist. We'd like you to have it, and this goes with it." Margaret reached into her bag and drew out a brochure and one of the bookmarks her mum's missionary guild had sewn with the reference for Romans 15:13 stitched on it. "You're also invited to our daily Bible study in the morning." She handed her a postcard with information about the study. "It will meet in our building just across the street. The office number is on the card. Tomorrow is the first one."

"Your office? I thought . . ."

"Yes," Graham spoke up. "We are finally in our office. In fact, we just met with the interior decorator to make a few final decisions, and tomorrow is our first official day working there. We'll have a grand opening at the end of next week. I'll be sure to send you an invitation."

"Okay." She looked down at the items she'd been given. "Thank you so much. Nice to meet you, Miss Elliot." She turned to Graham and inclined her head to him. "Good day, Mr. Corbyn." Shifting on her feet, Mrs. Brown walked back the way she'd come, only to stop and turn back around while shaking her head. She smiled at them and raised her shoulders as she passed.

Once she was out of earshot, Graham spoke. "Margaret, you were splendid."

"I honestly don't know where that came from, but I couldn't let her leave without showing her what she was missing out on."

"You did that and more. I'll have to start taking you everywhere with me. I'd already decided to look for someone else to answer the phones and do most of the typing."

She placed a hand on her hip. "You're replacing me?"

"I'm promoting you. I need a secretary, but you're more like my assistant."

"I noticed you called me that when introducing me to Mrs. Brown."

"I did. What do you think? You're doing the work of an assistant."

She bit back a smile. "Assistant. I think I like it. But maybe you should wait until things start to turn around and you have some income before hiring a new secretary."

He studied her before speaking. "What if I hire someone part-time to answer the phones and type—maybe two days a week? Then I can schedule you to come out with me on those days. Once things turn around for the company, I can hire a full-time secretary."

She rolled the idea around in her head. "Yes. I think that can work."

"And you can help me choose the secretary."

"Okay. But where will I work? I finally had my own space."

"This will be even better. You can have the private office next to mine. It has a window, so you'll still have plenty of sunlight."

"I do like sunlight." He'd been paying attention.

"Excellent. I'm glad we're agreed."

Just as they came to their agreement, the food arrived. What she'd thought would be a quick bite to satiate her hunger had turned into accolades and a promotion. If she wasn't careful, Graham would completely steal her heart. But she might not mind at all.

Half an hour later, they'd picked up their mail and returned to the Belgravia house, where Margaret sat down to work her last day in the library.

Graham sat at his desk going through the mail, and all seemed fine until he emphatically said, "What!"

"What is it, Graham?"

"I've received a letter from my former employer's solicitor telling me—in rather lofty terms—to stop doing something I've not even done."

"I don't understand."

"Neither do I, Margaret. Neither do I."

"Let me see. Maybe you're misinterpreting it."

"You are welcome to examine it, but the language is quite clear, even without legal training."

"Oh no. Surely it's a mistake." She walked over and sat down in the guest chair across from him at his desk.

"See for yourself. But yes, they are mistaken." Coming around the desk, he handed her the letter and stood over her.

The familiar scent of lemon and cardamom filled the air around them as she fought to focus on the words.

Dear Mr. Graham Corbyn,

We are instructed by our clients, Hall & Wright Ltd., in connection with recent concerns regarding certain authors, formerly or currently under contract with them, who have either received approaches from, or have entered into discussions with, your newly formed company, Corbyn Publishing Ltd.

You will be aware that under the terms of the agreement dated 17 May 1955, executed at the time of your departure from Hall & Wright Ltd., you undertook not to solicit, directly or indirectly, any author under active contract with our clients for a period of two years.

Our clients have reason to believe that communications initiated by

Corbyn Publishing Ltd. may constitute a breach of this undertaking. While we appreciate that your new venture is of a distinct editorial character, the overlapping of interests—whether by design or coincidence—raises legitimate concern.

We are therefore instructed to request, in the strongest terms, that you cease and desist from any further contact, correspondence, or negotiation with individuals under existing agreements with Hall & Wright Ltd., pending clarification of this matter.

Should it become evident that any breach has occurred, our clients reserve the right to pursue all legal remedies available to them, including injunctive relief and the recovery of damages.

We trust that this matter can be resolved without the need for further action and look forward to your written assurance that no such solicitations have taken place and that no further such contact will occur.

Yours faithfully,

C.A. Templeton, Esq.

She looked up and found him rubbing his chin. "That's quite a letter. I know you would never intentionally breach a contract, but is it possible you may have inadvertently contacted a few of their authors?"

"Absolutely not. I had them give me a list so I could be sure. I don't know what's going on."

"I think I do. Your company—"

"Our company, if it makes it through this." His brow was tightly knit as he rubbed across his face.

"Our company is under spiritual attack. Remember? You told me that yourself. It's because your plan is to build up Christian authors and help them share Jesus through their literary work."

A smile broke through his sadness, and he shook his head. "You're a wonder, Margaret."

"So we should pray."

"You're right. I don't know where to start. My mind is spinning."

"I'll pray. Christians are called to encourage and build one another up in 1 Thessalonians 5."

"Thank you. I do need that right now."

He followed her to the cushioned chairs, and she almost reached for his hand, something her family often did during prayer, but she stopped herself before he noticed.

"Let's pray. God, we have no idea what's going on here, but you do. Please protect our company from attacks of the evil one. You've made it clear that this company is part of your plan. Please protect it and give us direction here. Help us to glorify you even in this hard thing. Help us represent you well. If our company has done anything wrong, please bring it to light so we can make it right. If we have not, please make that abundantly clear. In Jesus' name. Amen."

"Thank you," he said softly, and when he lifted his head, she saw moisture in his eyes. "I'm going to call my solicitor, and I'll let you know what he says."

"Okay. I'll get back to work." She walked to her desk.

"If there's a company left to work for."

That had her attention. "Mr. Corbyn."

"Graham."

"No, you're acting like someone I barely know. Like I was saying, Mr. Corbyn, if you will remember, we just saw one of the authors who went to another publishing house and had a chance to encourage her. And you might not have noticed, but she seemed a little happier when she left. God is doing something here, and I don't think it's a coincidence that only a few minutes later, we opened this letter."

"You're right."

"So don't give up unless God makes it very clear you're supposed to,"

"Yes, ma'am." He hung his head, but she caught a gleam in his eye as he turned to his desk.

Sitting down at her own desk, she pulled out a thick sheet of paper and wrote down a verse, drew a quick sketch, then carefully cut it to pocket size. When Graham was done on the phone with his solicitor, she laid the verse in front of him.

"Our verse," he said after glancing at it. "Thanks. The butterfly you drew is a pretty addition." He laid it aside.

"Wait. Read it out loud."

Picking it back up, he studied it before reading. "May the God of hope fill you with all joy and peace in believing, so that by the power of the Holy Spirit, you may abound in hope." He looked up and pressed his lips together while nodding. "You're trying to tell me something."

"Yes." She reached for his Bible and flipped to Romans 15. "We haven't studied this in depth yet in our Bible study, but look at the context of the chapter. We Christians are to build one another up so that we can then share the gospel with unbelievers. It also reminds us that the steadfastness of God's words encourages us. Our task is not easy. God never promised that, and yet He called us to share him with the world. His word gives joy, peace, and hope."

Staring at the paper, he ran his fingers across the words. "Margaret, thank you for reminding me of my purpose and of why I started this company. Thank you for holding me to God's standard when I begin to doubt. I'm ashamed of myself."

"You had a moment of weakness. We are all tempted—it's what we do with those temptations that matters. That's also why we are to be in fellowship with other believers. We can bear one another's burdens and point each other to him when our burdens seem too great. You have been a great encouragement to me too. It's that give and take that God uses to keep us on track."

"I was just looking for a secretary, but God knew I would need so much more."

Chapter Eleven

Dinner was quieter that evening than they'd grown accustomed to, since Katie went to an after-work party. It had become the norm to stay and chat after dinner at Belgravia house. Mrs. Corbyn sat next to Margaret on a sofa doing needlework on a gift for a friend, and Graham sat beside them on a chair.

"I think I'll turn in early tonight," Mrs. Corbyn said as she folded up her needlework. "I had a long day helping with the church food pantry. Know that I'll be praying for you both with your work situation. Your solicitor seemed to think you'll have a good outcome, which leaves me hopeful. Goodnight, Margaret. Goodnight, Graham."

"Thank you. I'm hopeful too." Graham looked at Margaret. "A certain someone reminded me to be, and it helped. Goodnight, Mother."

"Goodnight, Mrs. Corbyn."

Mrs. Corbyn opened her mouth as if to speak but closed it and smiled as she turned and left.

"I've been wondering. Why the butterfly?" Graham pulled the paper with Romans 15:13 out of his pocket.

"It represents new life in Christ, the transformation we go through when becoming a Christian. Do you know the verse? 'Therefore, if anyone is in Christ, he is a new creation. The old has passed away; behold, the new has come.' It's 2 Corinthians 5:17. The butterfly and its concept of new life is a good representation of what yo—our company stands for and goes well with the verse. By the power of the Holy Spirit who helps us become something new, we have hope."

"I like that. Maybe we can make another version of the journal cover that has a butterfly. What do you think about adding it to that and some of our materials?"

"I think it's a wonderful idea. I'd love to see how you want to incorporate it."

"Thank you. I'll come up with some ways to use it and show you once I have them together."

She fiddled with her skirt as her thoughts drifted back to their day spent dealing with the letter from his former employer. Graham's solicitor planned to send out a letter the following day, listing the names of the people they had been in contact with and asking if any of them were on Hall & Wright's list unbeknownst to Graham. Margaret hoped that would settle things. Surely God wouldn't let the fledgling company fail when he'd called Graham to start it.

"Graham, you've never told me the full story of how God called you to start Corbyn Publishing."

"The full story?" He raised his brows. "Or the condensed version?"

"The full story, please."

"It started when my father was killed. Have you heard about how he died?"

Her chest tightened at his words. "No, I've not."

"Before his death, I'd planned to join my brother and father working for Corbyn Steel. I never felt particularly excited about it, but it was the family business. During the war, Corbyn Steel worked closely with the government to create steel for tanks, bullets, and other things necessary for the war effort. About a year before the end of the war, the government brought my dad and our company's metallurgist out to a recently liberated area to investigate armor failures in tanks. They were escorted by a military engineer who examined the area for land mines." He rubbed his face. "My father was killed by a landmine he missed.

"Between that and losing my sister before I was born, I decided my family had been through more than its share of misfortune. I was angry at God and angry at the world. I couldn't wait to join the military and take out my vengeance on someone. I became uninterested in the company, though I helped my brother some as he stepped up as head. Mostly, I withdrew and buried myself in books. I discovered C. S. Lewis's Space Trilogy and was intrigued with his writing. When I left for the army, I took his book, *The Problem of Pain*, and my mother slipped in a Bible. It talks about the very thing I was angry about. How could a good God be God if he allowed his people to go through difficulties? Lewis's strong logic had me straightened out in no time, and I began reading my Bible more earnestly than I ever had in my life. I got to the point that I needed his word to get me through each day.

"I also continued reading other books, both fiction and nonfiction —whatever I could get my hands on. In my search for good books, I saw the need for more that planted the seeds of the Christian faith. One day, it was almost as if I could hear God tell me to start a company and do that very thing."

"Kind of like when God spoke to us separately about the theme verse for the company?"

"Yes. Exactly like that. Once I finished my two years in the army and attended university, I planned to get experience working for another publisher and then begin my company. It fell into place, and here I am, wondering what God has next. Hoping it doesn't come to an end with a legal suit."

"We'll see, but I doubt he guided you so specifically for nothing."

"Thank you for your continual encouragement. I do need it. It's hard not to imagine the worst. And it saddens me to think my company, which is supposed to glorify God, is beginning with such a controversy around it."

"I agree. Maybe once Hall & Wright receives the letter from your solicitor, it will set things to right."

"I do hope so. Will you pray about it with me?"

"Of course. Would you like me to pray again?"

"I'll pray."

Once they bowed their heads, Graham prayed God would open the eyes of Hall & Wright to the truth and clear the name of Corbyn Publishing while glorifying himself.

After he said "Amen," Margaret thought back through their conversation and all he had been through. It saddened her to think of his losses. She knew firsthand what it was to lose a loved father.

"Graham, I'm truly sorry you lost your father. I know how hard that is."

"Yes, we do have that in common. The sadness about the loss never completely goes away, but God has comforted me time and again. I look forward to seeing my father again someday and even meeting my sister, Tracey." His eyes lifted to hers. "Have you found that comfort?"

"I have. It was a hard loss, but my family rallied around one another to get through. We were particularly focused on comforting my mum for the first few months, and it helped to have someone else to think about rather than dwelling on my own despondency. Eventually, I did take time to think more about my own feelings." A wave of sadness filled her, and she blinked back tears.

Graham reached out as if to wipe a tear from her cheek but quickly pulled it back before touching her. "Sorry, I . . . it pains me to see you so sad."

"I'll be okay. It resurfaces when I think of him, but I'm getting used to not having him around." She swiped at the errant tear. "I try to remember the happy times, and I do know he's much happier now, but sometimes I think of what he is missing and will miss in the future—the accomplishments of his children and watching his grandchildren continue to grow. I also think of what those grandchildren will miss out on. But mostly I just miss being able to talk to him and the wisdom that he shared with me. He was a good father."

"Those are familiar feelings for me. The sadness isn't as persistent as it was in the early days, but it's still an occasional interloper in my life."

"I'm sorry, Graham, for turning the conversation to something so depressing. I should be cheering you up."

"I don't always have to be cheery. There is a time for everything."

"Ecclesiastes."

"Yes, Margaret." A smile rose in contrast to his sad eyes. "You understand me. Let us hope that Hall & Wright does as well."

"Well, like Scarlett O'Hara says, tomorrow is another day."

On the first morning in the new office, as they gathered for Bible study, Margaret was filled with conflicting feelings. She was excited about the expansion of the company into the office, but the letter from Hall & Wright's solicitor loomed over them. Margaret, Graham, and Mrs. Corbyn were the only ones present who knew, and they all pasted on smiles.

As they showed the other employees the recently decorated office, a knock drew their attention to the door.

Graham opened it to find Mrs. Brown.

"Am I too late for the Bible study?" she asked.

"Of course not. Welcome." Graham introduced her to the staff before they gathered in the conference room to read some verses from Romans and introduce their theme verse along with the mission for Corbyn Publishing.

Mrs. Brown listened intently and answered one of the questions Graham asked while reviewing their passage. The intense look on her face gradually relaxed into a pleasant look of satisfaction.

At the end of the study, she cornered Graham and Margaret and said, "I just had to come and see things for myself. I didn't like thinking ill of you when your company seemed so promising. I do admire the mission, but I'd been led to doubt it. I still haven't fully committed myself to the other company. I probably shouldn't be telling you this, but I will be visiting your studies this week and will reconsider based on how I feel God is leading me."

Graham's face transformed from concern to delight. "Thank you for giving us another chance, Mrs. Brown. I don't take that lightly."

After Mrs. Brown left, Margaret and Graham beamed at one another.

"You did it," they said simultaneously.

"I think we can agree that God did it through us. If Mrs. Brown does indeed return to us, that is."

"If the determining factor is how she feels about our integrity and commitment to our mission after attending our Bible study, I can't imagine she wouldn't want to join us," Margaret said. By the way he furrowed his brow, she could tell doubt was creeping in. "Graham, you are a good leader for this company, and if she is around you any amount of time, she will see that and your commitment to directing this company towards God."

"Thank you for the encouragement. With the authors leaving and the Hall & Wright accusation, I'm beginning to doubt myself."

She reached out and squeezed his upper arm. "Stand firm, Graham. God has a plan."

He nodded as his eyes drifted to where her hand rested on his arm. His brow furrowed.

"I'm so sorry." Heat rose to her face, and she snatched her hand back. She was getting entirely too familiar with him. Maybe she should call him Mr. Corbyn again. Turning quickly, she rushed to the reception area but heard footsteps behind her.

"Margaret, it's fine. You're a good friend. It just . . . caught me off guard."

"I won't make that mistake again, sir." She sat down behind the desk.

"Mar—Miss Elliot." Graham stepped away from her as another employee walked past. "Would you please come to my office?"

"Shouldn't I stay here to answer the phone?"

"The phone will have to wait. I'll be quick."

She nodded and followed him to his office.

"This Margaret at home and Miss Elliot here business is difficult."

"We'll figure it out, I'm sure. What did you need me for?"

"I didn't want to leave things unsettled with you. As for the back and forth of the names, it is going to be difficult because we have become friends and have not had to face the worry of whether our actions seemed appropriate, considering our working relationship. But here, I suppose everything will be under scrutiny. I don't want things to be awkward. As we should with everything, we can pray for wisdom. And for now, at work, we should stick to Mr. and Miss."

"Certainly. I will do that. Thank you . . . Mr. Corbyn." She turned to leave.

"Margaret. Are you upset?"

"Of course not, sir." She forced a smile, but the whole situation was awkward. "I'm just hurrying to my desk in case anyone needs me there."

The reception area was busy the first day with deliveries of office supplies and people coming by to see the new office. Mostly friends and family visited, since the official open house wasn't scheduled until the following week.

Until Graham hired a new secretary, Margaret agreed to continue in that position, but it was hard to follow through with her ideas for the company when she was tied up answering the phone, greeting, and escorting people around. Although today, she was glad to have the position so she could answer the phone if the solicitor called or receive his correspondence. The solicitor had a courier take their letter to Hall & Wright's solicitor first thing that morning, and they were hoping for a quick response.

It was just after four in the evening when Graham's solicitor, Mr. Davies, called back. Graham invited Margaret to wait in his office while he was on the phone so he could immediately share their response, but from his furrowed brow and rapid scribbling, she knew something was wrong.

Once he hung up the phone, he sighed and rubbed a hand over his face. He closed his eyes before looking up and shaking his head. "I don't understand, but they said they had a hundred more names on their list, but those names weren't on the list they gave me, and seventy-three of those hundred were ones that I have contacted. Seventy-three! It doesn't make any sense. How do they have a hundred additional names? I have the paper with their letterhead that doesn't list those hundred names."

"Graham—I mean, Mr. Corbyn." She shook her head in frustration. At a time like this, the challenge of a new name was one more thing to sift through. "I'm so sorry. There must be some mistake."

He stared at her with a blank stare as if she were a stranger. "There is, but I don't know how to prove it. My solicitor says he can take my original list as proof, but beyond that, we're both at a loss."

Margaret silently prayed as he spoke, asking God to give him direction and show her how to encourage him. An idea sparked. "Does your solicitor have the list of the seventy-three names we contacted?"

"I'm not sure."

"I'd like to see the list."

"Me too." He moved from behind his desk and began pacing. "How did they leave out one hundred names? I'd like to see *that* list. I wonder if those hundred are people they've removed from their files because they no longer do business with them and now there's confusion. Or maybe they didn't start doing business with them until after I left."

"It could be so many things. It would be wonderful if it's as simple as that. I'll pray before you call the solicitor back."

"Thank you, but I'd like to pray this time. I think I'm more clear-headed than when I first found out yesterday," he said.

They both bowed their heads as Graham prayed for wisdom and patience with this situation.

After praying, Graham called the solicitor back. The solicitor didn't have a copy of the list of hundred but only seventy-three. He suggested they set up an appointment for the following day to go to Hall & Wright and review the lists and discuss things with them.

Chapter Twelve

Six. Six authors, out of the seventy-three on Hall & Wright's list, currently had contracts with Corbyn Publishing.

Hall & Wright was now officially proceeding with a lawsuit. Graham and Margaret kept busy in their effort to contact the six to find out if they had indeed been under contract with or in negotiations with Hall & Wright. Most of Corbyn Publishing's authors resided outside of London or on the continent, so communication was slow. After their first attempt at calling, they'd only reached two of the authors and still had no answers. One said he'd recently been in contact with a company that was elusive, only referring to themselves as H. W. Press. The other said she'd been in negotiations with Hall & Wright years before but had never signed with them. That was one decisive testimony in their favor.

Graham, Mrs. Corbyn, and Margaret sat in his office, discussing the situation.

"Mr. Davies is working on getting written statements from the two, but they live out of town. It will be days before the testimonies are in hand. Hall & Wright still won't budge, even with Mr. Davies's verbal affirmation of the response from our two clients," Graham said.

"The staff is beginning to wonder what all of the private meetings are about." Mrs. Corbyn twisted her hands in her lap from Graham's lounge chair. She'd taken over as secretary in the reception area to allow Margaret extra time to help Graham.

"Should I tell them that their jobs are in jeopardy?" Graham's frown and furrowed brow displayed his worry.

"I feel like God wants you to hold off—like something is going to come to light and he will make things right." Mrs. Corbyn stood up and walked to her son, placing a hand on his shoulder. "I don't think it's just the mother in me wanting you to succeed. I'd like to call my prayer chain and have them pray for you. I won't tell them why. Would you mind?"

"Of course not, Mother. We can certainly use God's intervention." He looked at Margaret. "Thoughts?"

"I think she's right. I think it will be a stressful process getting to the bottom of this, but I also believe God wants us to see this through and not give up."

Graham sighed. "Okay." He closed his eyes and pursed his lips. When he opened his eyes, he said, "I'm giving it one week. If by next Tuesday there hasn't been any movement in our direction, I will tell the staff on Wednesday. We currently have only four contracts that aren't with authors who are on the list. That's not enough to support full-time staff. I won't have my employees ruin their prospects by staying with a company that may fail."

Mrs. Corbyn nodded slowly. "Okay, but I do think God will come through."

"Thank you for your encouragement and help, Mother. I know you have other things you'd rather be doing yourself than giving so much time here." He stood and stepped back from his desk.

"There's no place I'd rather be than helping one of my boys. I'll head back up front before the staff wonders why I've disappeared too." Mrs. Corbyn hugged Graham and slipped out of the room.

"Do you really think we'll come out of this, Miss Elliot?"

Margaret wanted to wince at the sound of "Miss Elliot" when they were in the privacy of his office, but this wasn't the time to get emotional. He needed her help, and though she secretly wished she'd been placed in his orbit for more than just helping with the start of Corbyn Publishing, it might be the only reason God placed her here.

"I do," she found herself saying. And she did think they would. As for her part, she would do everything in her power to see to it that Graham Corbyn succeeded in getting through this with the publishing company intact. The world needed a publisher who worked to put out books that glorified God and get them into the hands of as many people as possible. *God, give us both wisdom and show me how I can help him. Help me to push my distracting thoughts away so I can focus on the task at hand.* "Let's send some telegrams. They'll get to the authors we haven't been able to contact faster than letters."

Pacing and tapping his chin, Graham stopped. "I like that. If you wouldn't mind, I'll dictate a message to you. Then a driver can take you to the telegram office, and you can send the same message to the other four authors."

"I'd be happy to. I've already pulled their addresses."

Margaret lifted her eyes to find Graham walking towards her Belgrave Square garden spot with a smile and determination in his eyes.

"What is it?" Margaret questioned. "Do you need me back at the office?" Her lunch breaks in the park became a means of escape and refreshment over the last week. Some of her best ideas came while she was there—ideas for reaching out to more authors.

"We have them all," he said as he joined her on the blanket.

"All of the six authors?"

"Yes, and none of them are in contract at present with Hall & Wright. The last two said they've never been in contract with Hall & Wright."

"Wonderful! So three have never been in contract with them." She counted on her fingers. "Two had contracts on past books but no longer do, and the other has spoken to a company calling itself H. W. Press but did not sign a contract."

"Exactly. And we have it all on signed affidavits from them. They've been couriered over to Hall & Wright's legal offices."

"And you've added two more new authors to our list of authors in contract?"

"We did, Miss Elliot."

She'd stopped correcting him when he referred to her that way outside of the office. "So . . . no need to tell the staff? Things are looking positive."

"I'm hesitant to say our worries are over, but . . . things are looking up."

"Good. Have a biscuit and enjoy a few minutes of not thinking about lists and contracts."

"That sounds amazing." He held his hand open for a biscuit, and Margaret placed it on his palm. As he closed his fingers around it, they brushed against Margaret's, and his eyes caught hers. His smile melted into something more serious.

Tingles radiated up her arm, and her heart nearly beat out of her chest. Neither moved. Did he feel what she did?

Something small moved in her peripheral vision.

"Look. It's one of your butterflies," Graham said, and her gaze followed his.

A soothing blue-colored butterfly alighted on a picnic blanket. It was a beautiful sight. "He has made everything beautiful in its time." Margaret looked back at Graham.

"Also he has put eternity into man's mind, yet so that he cannot find out what God has done from the beginning to the end. Ecclesiastes 3:11." His words finished her thought, and her heart leaped.

He was so perfectly matched to her—how could they not be intended for one another?

The colors of the nearby garden seemed to brighten and come alive with the joy that filled her. She glanced up. Had the sun peeked from behind a cloud? It had not, yet the weight she'd felt before Graham arrived with his news had lifted.

"We should celebrate," she said.

"I agree. Perhaps I'll have Cook make a special dinner tonight, or maybe have a night out on the town," Graham offered.

"A simple dinner in is fine, but maybe we can plan something more fun for the weekend. Katie and I were saying we'd love to visit a beach along the Channel. It's an area we've not been to."

"Brilliant. Let's do it. I'll talk it over with Mother. She has a friend, Mrs. Price, who has a cottage in Kingsdown. Maybe we can use it for the day."

"I've never heard of Kingsdown. What is it close to?"

"It's just north of Dover. A quaint area with fewer crowds than other beaches."

"That's what I'd prefer. I'll talk it over with Katie."

"It sounds like we have a plan." He looked at his watch before standing up. "Now it is time to get back to the office. I'm afraid I've taken up your break again."

"It was more than worth it."

He helped her pack up her lunch and return the basket to the house before they turned back to walk to the office. The entire way, her heart fluttered as they walked in step with one another. Both remained quiet. For her part, she was drinking in his presence.

Mrs. Corbyn grinned from behind the reception desk as they entered the office together. "It's wonderful news, is it not?"

"Indeed, it is." Margaret peeked at Graham. "Things are looking up."

Half an hour before closing, Graham knocked on her open office door, a frown on his face and his normally perfect posture slumped.

"Bad news."

From behind her desk, she said a silent prayer that it had nothing to do with the legal case.

"I've received a telegram from one of the authors I told you about at lunch, who had just said he wanted to sign with us. He has backed out. And another author who had signed with us has requested annulment of the contract. Our solicitor says that since no money has been exchanged, we shouldn't hold him to it. It would be an extensive and costly legal battle."

Margaret's heart dropped. *What does this mean, God?* "I'm so sorry. I don't know what to say." Were the legal case and loss of authors somehow tied together? Had word spread that they were embroiled in a legal battle?

"There's nothing to say. It's time to admit defeat."

"You're telling the other employees? So they can look for other work?"

"Yes, but I also think you should look for something else. I can put in a good word for you with Hall & Wright. It may not be a Christian publishing company, but they do work with Christian authors, and many of the people in charge are Christians. They'll be good to you."

"You're closing the company?"

"Yes." The finality in his voice made her heart sink.

How could this be happening? God had blessed so much of what they'd done. He'd given them a plan and a verse. He'd helped them contact the six and add two—now one—additional author. But they had lost another one.

And yet she didn't want to make Graham feel guilty. If pushing past this setback was more than he could bear, she would help him by not making it any harder. She forced a smile.

"Okay. I'll help you do whatever you decide." She hoped he would change his mind.

"You don't agree?"

"I . . . I want to support you in your decision."

He nodded and abruptly turned to leave.

"But I do think God might surprise you," she said before he opened the door. "He made himself clear before—about you starting the publishing company for him."

"I thought he had. Yet here we are."

"Here we are." Standing, she met him by the door. She looked into his eyes and held his gaze, hoping he would take back his words.

For a moment, his eyes softened, and she thought he might take back his earlier pronouncement.

"I'll meet you in the reception area at five thirty to walk you home. I'll make the announcement in the morning." He did leave this time.

The following morning, birds seemed to mock Margaret with their chirping as she walked alongside Graham to Corbyn Publishing—so he could announce that the company would soon close. His mother tried convincing him to give it more of a chance, but he remained firm. He wouldn't risk the livelihoods of others for his own vanity. He was an honorable man, and each day, she admired him more.

Looking up, her eyes traced Graham's silhouette. He was a hand-some man—the most handsome man she knew, inside and out. Would things be different if she was no longer working with him? Might he view her differently if he was no longer her boss? Maybe he would allow himself to pursue her then.

He turned his head and caught her staring. Time seemed to slow. Had the three blocks grown to ten? It would be just as well if they never arrived. Maybe she could feign illness and turn back.

Graham stopped. "Margaret, thank you for all you've done for Corbyn Publishing. You are the most talented woman I know in the publishing world. I meant it when I said I would put in a good word for you. And I don't only mean for a job. I'll also promote your books with them. Don't lose your fire for writing."

"Thank you."

"I'm sorry for bringing you here and letting you down. But I have been praying about this, and it's the right thing to do."

"And this is what God told you to do?"

He shrugged. "He hasn't told me not to. I feel responsible for the people who work for me, and I won't wait until the last minute and leave them without work. I'll do references for all of them."

"What will *you* do once the company closes?"

"I'll work for my brother at Corbyn Steel."

"I thought you hated that type of office work."

"I . . . I don't need to do it for the money, but I refuse to be a man of leisure. God created man for work, and I am trained for it."

"You're an honorable man, Graham."

He glanced up at the office building before looking back at her and holding out his arm. "Shall we?"

She nodded but had no more words. Taking his arm, she followed him into the building and up to their office. Everything around them dimmed as dread filled her.

Graham opened the door, and she walked through reluctantly.

The first face she saw was Mrs. Brown's. Margaret had completely forgotten about the morning Bible study and had failed to call and tell her it was canceled.

"Mrs. Brown. Good . . . to see you." Margaret stumbled over her words.

"Miss Elliot, Mr. Corbyn. So good to see you both." She looked at Graham. "Mr. Corbyn, may I speak with you privately?"

"Of course." Graham escorted her to his office.

Margaret couldn't tell from her facial expression what she might say, but began praying.

Nearly five minutes later they came out—both smiling.

"Mrs. Brown has decided she will join the Corbyn Publishing family after all," Graham said.

Margaret watched Graham for a sign as to what it meant for the company, but she couldn't tell. They followed Graham into the conference room and had Bible study. Afterwards, Mrs. Brown left, and Graham waved Margaret into his office.

"What—"

"I'm keeping Corbyn Publishing open. When I saw Mrs. Brown, I felt God saying, 'See, I'm not finished here.' I can't close it. He's working in it, and I will see it through, even if I have to pay employees out of my own pocket."

A rush of joy filled her. She'd hoped for a change such as this and had even asked God for it. She had begun to doubt it was his plan, yet here they were moving forward again with the company.

"I feel foolish for not trusting God in this. He has shown himself faithful time and again. It seems I had more to learn about his faithfulness." Graham paced his office. "I should have listened to you. Please forgive me for doubting. I've said it before—he put you in my life for a reason. I will try not to forget again." Stopping next to her, he said, "I do want to go out of town this weekend. I'll talk to Mother and see if she can set it up to go to Kingsdown."

"Wonderful. I look forward to it."

Chapter Thirteen

Friday evening, as they rounded the corner on a gravel coastal road in Kingsdown, Margaret caught a glimpse of the water in the English Channel. She could just make out the beach huts lined up facing the water. A few people strolled along a pathway that stretched past the homes with beach views.

They pulled to a stop outside the gate of a two-story whitewashed, hip-roofed cottage with upper-level balconies.

"This is it," Graham said to Mrs. Corbyn, Margaret, and Katie. "Wait in the car, and I'll open the gate and pull the car through."

As they pulled past the gate, a lovely front garden came into view just before he pulled into the garage.

"I've had someone stop by and bring cold cuts, vegetables, fruit, and such for us. But we may want to take a short walk to view the coast before the sun goes down. We have nearly an hour before then. What would the rest of you like to do?"

Katie looked at Margaret, and they both said "Beach!" at the same time.

"A walk along the coast it is," announced Graham.

Minutes later, Margaret and Katie had settled their luggage in an upstairs bedroom with a view of the garden below—pink roses and lavender bloomed among other flowers.

"Katie, look." Margaret pointed to the garden as she sat on a bench beneath the window.

Katie joined her. "How lovely! I can't believe this is our view for the whole weekend. What a treat."

"Indeed! Gardens, beaches, castles . . ." Margaret thought about all the options Mrs. Corbyn had suggested they visit.

Margaret and Katie changed shoes and met the others by the door.

Graham opened the door and held out an arm to help his mother down the stairs.

She shooed him. "Graham, dear, you're making me feel old. I can manage with the railing just fine. If anything, be a gentleman and help the young ladies. They're more likely to appreciate it than me, and you can use the practice."

Graham's face turned pink as he moved towards Margaret and Katie, holding out both arms. When Graham looked down, Katie wiggled her eyebrows at Margaret. She rolled her eyes.

Katie had not pressured Margaret about Graham in the several weeks since she told her she no longer thought it was a good idea to consider Graham romantically. Not that there wasn't a tug at her heart, but how could she be anything more than the young sister of his friend with such an age gap? He was years ahead of her in experience, and what would his friends and family think?

She wrapped her arm around one of his and pushed the thoughts down despite her racing heart. *God, take this from me.*

A couple arm-in-arm with two children skipping ahead passed just before they entered the path. They looked so happy together. It was the idyllic life Margaret had not allowed herself to think about ever since John had rejected her. She followed the family's progress until she heard "Ahem."

Looking up, she found Graham staring down at her. Katie had already released his other arm and was walking behind them alongside Mrs. Corbyn.

"Sorry. The children had me distracted." The excuse sounded flimsy even to her own ears.

"I thought you intended to remain single and not have children? It seems you have a soft spot for little ones."

"Can't I remain single *and* enjoy children?"

"You can." He frowned and turned to watch the water lap against the beach.

She didn't like the tightness in her chest that arose after telling him she'd remain single. Taking a deep breath, she let the sea air cleanse her thoughts.

"May we go down and walk on the beach?" she asked, aching to get closer to the water.

"Certainly." Graham sped up and touched Mrs. Corbyn's arm. "Would you like to walk along the water, Mother? Katie?"

"I'd rather not, dear. In fact, I'd quite like to head back. I can set out some food for when all of you return." Mrs. Corbyn patted Graham on the arm.

"I actually think I'll head back with you, Mrs. Corbyn," offered Katie.

"Thank you, dear. It would be nice to have the company."

Graham and Margaret waved at the two as they left for the cottage. Silence lingered between Graham and Margaret as they turned and walked along the coast. Thoughts echoed in Margaret's head until she had to speak.

"This is a lovely beach. The sea breeze always refreshes me." It wasn't what she really wanted to say, but it was a start.

Graham nodded in her direction but made no reply.

A family played with their young son and cocker spaniel ahead of them. The woman turned and revealed an obvious baby bump.

Graham glanced at her with downcast eyes, and she instantly felt sad.

She couldn't hold her question back any longer. "Do you want a family and children one day?"

"I do." He left the words hanging as they passed the family with the dog.

Several times she opened her mouth to speak but felt unsure about what to say.

"I was engaged once." Graham's shoulders hunched. "While I was away in the army, she married someone else."

"You weren't expecting it? Did she not write to you that she was having doubts or wanted out of the relationship?"

"Her letter got to me after she had already married him. It was a hard way to find out, though I had begun to question our relationship when her letters became further apart."

"I'm so sorry. So you understand some of what I've been through."

He nodded, and her heart ached for him.

"And it didn't make you want to remain single?"

"On the contrary, it made me want marriage more."

"I see." Except she didn't. How was it that being jilted made him more determined to marry, but it made her wary of men who made her hope for something they never intended to give?

He stopped and stooped down, grabbing a pebble and skipping it across the water. Her eyes followed his movements, and her heart raced.

"Have you heard from your mother recently? How is she doing?" he asked.

"I received a letter from her yesterday. She says she's adjusting to life in Arthur's home and enjoying all of the extra time with my nephews and niece."

"I'm glad to hear it." The muscles in his jaw tightened.

She wondered if he was thinking of the legal case that still continued. They'd agreed to take the weekend off from worrying about it or discussing it, but it still hovered around the edges of her thoughts. Surely it had the same hold over him.

"Arthur's daughter, Clara, was sick, and that took up much of the letter too."

Graham turned to her with furrowed brows. "Sick?"

"She's fine now. It was just a head cold."

"Good. That's good." His face relaxed. "With what happened to my sister . . ."

She nodded in understanding.

The breeze sent a chill across her skin as the sun eased closer to the horizon.

"Take my jacket." Graham pulled his jacket off and held it out.

As she slipped on his suit jacket, the familiar scent of lemon, neroli, and cardamom swirled around her. The combination fit him perfectly

—uplifting and comforting with a warmth that grounded her. She wanted to bury her face in the jacket. If he weren't right beside her, she might have.

"Thank you." In her delirium, she'd almost forgotten her manners. Lately, just being in his presence was a balm for her soul.

"Margaret, you are a blessing, dear," Mrs. Corbyn said as she stirred her morning tea.

Katie had not come down yet, and Graham had gone for an early morning walk while Margaret breakfasted with Mrs. Corbyn.

"You're mistaken. Your family has been a blessing to me. My job at Corbyn Publishing is better than any I had imagined finding in the publishing world. And to have my housing taken care of and be treated as family is more than I ever expected."

"I am glad to hear it, but I was referring to your being a blessing to Graham. You are what he needs in his life—not just in business, but also in his personal life."

That had her attention. "What do you mean?"

Mrs. Corbyn tilted her head and pressed her lips together before speaking. "Did you know Graham was engaged once?"

Margaret's heart rate sped up. "He mentioned it to me yesterday."

Mrs. Corbyn's brow rose. "He did? Well, I'm guessing he didn't mention that she was a fortune hunter."

Margaret shook her head.

"She was. When Graham decided not to keep working at Corbyn Steel and instead start his own company after the army, she went and found herself someone she thought had better financial prospects for the future. Graham would never say anything hurtful about her, but it's the truth."

Sitting a little taller in her seat, Margaret contemplated the news. His situation was more similar to hers than she'd realized. Though in her situation, John never believed she had money, and it was only after his family influenced his thinking that he changed his mind about a relationship with her.

"I understand what that's like."

"So I've heard, and I'm quite sorry. But I believe God was preserving you both for someone better."

She was tempted to say she didn't feel she had to marry but instead said, "Maybe." In truth, she wasn't entirely convinced anymore that she could be happy as a single woman. Maybe applying herself more thoroughly to work and ministry would rid her of those feelings.

"Graham is great about going after the things he feels God has directed him to, like with Corbyn Publishing, but ever since Violet, the former fiancée who jilted him, he's been slower to move forward in romantic relationships. There have been women he considered courting since things ended with her, but he hesitates and second-guesses himself. The women always move on before he speaks up."

As Mrs. Corbyn spoke, Margaret could hardly believe she might be implying that she and Graham were meant for one another. Surely she was misunderstanding. But a tiny—maybe large—part of her wanted to believe it. "Why are you telling me this?"

"Because I've seen the way Graham looks at you and you look at him. There's a great deal of respect . . . but also something more. I hope you don't think me impertinent, and if I'm mistaken, you can take this all with a grain of salt, but it seems you and Graham are made for one another. I hope you'll be patient with him. It might not hurt to help him see he has a chance with you. Give him some encouragement."

"I'm not . . . I don't think—"

"Not in an overt way, of course, because that would be unlike you." Mrs. Corbyn tapped her chin. "God will guide you."

Heat rose to Margaret's face at the idea. Was she so obvious in her attention towards him? A few times, she'd thought she saw interest in Graham's eyes, but she'd always told herself it stemmed from his friendship with her brother. "I hardly know what to say, ma'am."

"I'm sorry if I've embarrassed you, but I can't get through to Graham when I touch on the subject, and I don't want you to slip away from him. I'm too old to waste any more time. You are just what he needs. I've seen the way your talents and personality fit with his. You are both following the Lord and attempting to please him, not men. That is a rarity nowadays. I see that you are sincere in your love for God above all else, and Graham sees it too. That's why he's trusted you in all of this."

"In the legal situation with Hall & Wright?"

"Yes, and with trying to keep from losing more authors. I've seen much in my years on this earth. Some people will go to extraordinary lengths for money and power. It drives them to destroy everyone and everything in their path. Violet is on that path, and from what I've heard, she's reaping the results of her choices." She shook her head slowly.

"The war is a large-scale example of that misplaced drive. Hitler was motivated by a hunger for power. It's that hunger that cost my husband and many others their lives. Its evil radiated outward and caused so much more evil.

"When my husband died, some of the Corbyn Steel executives tried to undermine the company and wrestle it from my son James by discrediting him. They were men we trusted and whom I never would have believed could stoop to such measures, chasing after personal glory and riches. I've experienced what the desire to raise oneself up through money and power does, and I've worked hard to see that, despite our money, my boys use it as a tool for God's glory and not theirs. You have that same zeal to give God glory."

"I . . . thank you, ma'am. I don't feel worthy for you to say such things." Margaret knew her own imperfections. God knew her imperfections.

"And that is exactly why I think you are perfect for Graham. I'm trying not to meddle. I know young people have to make these decisions for themselves, but I think both of you underestimate your worthiness for the other. I taught Graham long ago to follow God's lead as to what he should do. I never wanted him to feel tied to Corbyn Steel. As Christians, we can represent God in whatever work we go into, but God's ways are filled with order and logic, and I believe if we are seeking after him, he will show us what he has gifted us for. Graham and you are both made for the publishing world, and I love the way you encourage one another in that. You make a good team. I trust you will pray about this, of course. Choosing a spouse is even more important than choosing a job." Mrs. Corbyn's calm countenance belied the seriousness of the topic.

Margaret, on the other hand, was sure her wide-eyed expression gave away her surprise and confusion. Did Mrs. Corbyn truly think she was an appropriate choice for marriage with Graham? She was simultaneously delighted at the thought and scared of risking her feelings.

Mrs. Corbyn drank her last sip of tea, dabbed her mouth, and stood. She stepped to Margaret and touched her shoulder. "Follow God's lead, and you'll be fine. I'm praying for you both." She turned to step away but hesitated and looked back. "Oh, and one more thing. I think it quite odd that Corbyn Publishing is simultaneously losing authors to another publishing company and being sued over stealing authors from Hall & Wright. I'm inclined to believe they are tied together. And perhaps the person behind it all is someone close we would never suspect. Money and power, dear—it's all about money and power."

Margaret blinked as she took in her words. "I believe you might be right. I've begun to have a similar thought but had not mentioned it to Graham yet. We promised one another we wouldn't discuss the legal case this weekend."

The edges of Mrs. Corbyn's mouth curled up just before she said, "Quite right," then turned away.

"I still can't believe she wants me as a daughter-in-law," Margaret said as she clipped another rose from the cottage garden and handed it to Katie. Mrs. Corbyn's friend had told her they could cut all the roses they wanted in the garden. Her friend had not used her beach home in months and said they needed trimming anyway. Margaret was delighted to make bouquets to place around the cottage and fill it with the scent of roses.

"I can. It's obvious you two are perfect for each other."

"That's basically what she said. But you know me—I don't know how to begin showing him I want more with him. I'm so awkward when it comes to romance. It's a miracle John was ever interested in me. If we'd not grown up together, I don't think he would have been. And are Graham and I right for each other, or do I just seem to be what he needs because we work together and are both interested in books? Maybe I'm too young and naive? Maybe he needs someone more mature and experienced in life."

"I disagree about you being awkward. Maybe you don't bat your eyelashes like me." She fluttered her lashes and giggled at her joke. "But you are your real self around him. You—ouch." Katie drew her hand away from the rosebush and examined her hand. "The thorns on these things hurt." She wiped a drop of blood off her finger. "What was I saying? Oh, yes. You talk a lot to him, and you've created a bond through your mutual interests. It's that bond that makes it something special. And, no, I don't think he needs someone more mature. You are like an old woman in a young woman's body. You always have been."

"What does that mean?" Margaret's hands landed on her hips. "It doesn't sound very flattering. He may not need a woman as young as myself, but I doubt he wants an old woman either." She scrunched up her face.

Katie chuckled. "I mean it in the best way. You're very introspective and thoughtful like someone beyond your years. From what I've seen, it works well with his personality."

"Thank you, I guess."

"And regarding how to show him you are interested, just remember —there's no need to rush things like Mrs. Corbyn seems to be implying. Just let the relationship evolve naturally, like you're doing. She's likely in a hurry to have more grandchildren."

A rustle nearby drew their attention. It was Graham, and Margaret wondered how much of their conversation he'd overheard.

"Mother sent me out with this basket to put the cut roses in."

His cheeks were pink, confirming Margaret's guess that he'd heard something.

"Wonderful," Katie said as she laid them in the basket. "I'm having a time holding onto them with their thorns." She held out her previously injured finger, and Graham looked closely at it. "Trust me. There was blood there, and I wiped it off."

"Do you need ointment?" Graham asked.

"I think I do." Katie handed him the basket. "You can help Margaret finish up here while I see to my wound." She winked at Margaret from behind his back as she walked off.

Suddenly Margaret's mind was blank. Should she be mad at Katie for leaving them or thankful? The pressure to woo him as Mrs. Corbyn wanted unnerved her, and the temperature seemed to rise. "It's a lovely day out." She smiled up at him while internally chastising herself for saying something so mundane.

One corner of his mouth rose. "It is. You seem rather enamored with these flowers."

"I am. I helped tend the garden at our home in Steventon. It was one of my favorite things to do. I've always liked roses. They can be finicky to grow, but with proper care, the results are beautiful."

"You'll enjoy the gardens at Walmer Castle then."

"I'm looking forward to it. Your mother mentioned the garden there is lovely. Do you do any gardening?"

"I've never had a green thumb, though truthfully, I haven't taken the time to learn. Maybe you can teach me a few things. I'm sure Mother would let you add some flowers of your choice to the garden at our Belgravia house."

"Would she? I would like that. It already has a lovely garden, and I would be honored to help with it."

As she turned to hand him a clipped rose, she noticed the ruffling of a curtain in the cottage and thought she caught a glimpse of Mrs. Corbyn.

"When everyone is ready, we can go to lunch at Ye Olde Shrieking Peach before our visit to the castle. It's an old tavern that's been around for ages and a must when visiting the area if you want an authentic feel."

"Oh?" Seeing his mother had distracted Margaret, and she wasn't sure what he'd said. "I'm sorry. Did you say something about peaches?"

He chuckled. "They do have quite a few items with peaches on their menu. I said Ye Olde Shrieking Peach. It's a Kingsdown institution. It's been here for years, and I thought we could go eat lunch there before going to the castle."

"I trust your judgement. I do want to get an authentic feel for the area."

"While we're in town, we should also go to the Rose and Crown. It's a pub that serves good food. They have an excellent Sunday roast."

"That sounds like a perfect plan."

Chapter Fourteen

As Margaret stood at her file cabinet putting papers away in her office Monday morning, her thoughts drifted to the weekend. The getaway was wonderful, and in some ways, she'd never wanted it to end. She'd had some moments with Graham that she hoped helped him to see her as more than an employee and friend, but another part of her was anxious to get back to the real world so they could work towards figuring out who was taking their authors and who was framing them at Hall & Wright. Were they tied together? She'd thought about it sporadically throughout the weekend—when she wasn't distracted with thoughts of Graham and whether she should pursue him and what she should do to show him she wanted more.

Pushing the file drawer closed, she leaned back against it and conjured up those beautiful blue eyes she'd grown attached to. He was dreamy, and it was hard not to think of him even when he wasn't around. He'd gone out for a meeting, and she didn't expect him back until after lunch. More and more, she found herself missing him whenever they were apart.

If they did get into a romantic relationship, would it change their working relationship? Should she look for another job? She adored Corbyn Publishing, not just the man behind it, and she doubted there was another company that could even begin to compare with it.

She'd heard of companies not allowing dating relationships among coworkers. They'd not discussed that. She imagined it might be challenging to separate a working relationship from a professional one. Katie assured her they would be able to figure out how to make it work, but Katie was just as new to the working world as she was. Ever since Mrs. Corbyn spoke to her, Margaret had been praying about a possible relationship with Graham and what she should do.

A sound in Graham's office caught her attention, and she wondered why he'd returned so early. Blushing at her previous thoughts, she composed herself and walked next door to check on him. She also wanted to talk over her theories about their two business situations.

Approaching the door, she found it open several inches. Not wanting to barge in, she peeked through the crack and raised her hand to knock. Instead of seeing Graham, she saw his friend Charles Sutton. He was leaning over the desk and scribbling something on paper. She began to turn away and not disturb him while he wrote his note for Graham, but a thought hit her, and she froze.

She scanned the desk and noted a small paper bag sitting on it that was not there earlier. Mr. Sutton regularly brought Graham treats from local diners, so that wasn't unusual. Her attention turned back to him as his left hand ran across what looked like Graham's daily planner and he continued writing in a notebook with his other hand. When he paused, she pulled away, heart beating wildly. Was he . . . surely not.

Slipping quietly back into her own office, she stood just inside the door, listening for sounds that Mr. Sutton was leaving. It was several minutes more before she heard the rustle and squeak of Graham's door. She looked through her cracked door and saw Mr. Sutton sliding his notebook into his jacket pocket as he pulled the door closed and walked down the hall.

Margaret let out a shaky breath. Now she was more anxious than ever to talk to Graham, though he might not appreciate his friend's veracity being questioned. "God, please show me—show us—what is true and what we need to know in all of this," she whispered as she settled into her desk chair.

Before pulling out her work, she took a mental inventory of the times she'd seen Mr. Sutton or heard of his interactions with Graham since she'd begun working for him. He often came to visit Graham when he was out for work or on break. When they worked from the Belgravia house, there were three times she remembered him dropping by when Graham wasn't there. Once, when she was at her desk, he left a slice of cake and wrote a note for Graham. Two other times, she was eating lunch at her usual spot in the garden of Belgrave Square and spotted him carrying a bag into the home and leaving a few minutes later. Were there other times she might not have seen him? Should she even be suspecting him of something nefarious? She recalled an uncomfortable feeling the first day she met him, on the day of her interview, and thinking him quite forward, considering she was a stranger, but she'd assumed her discomfort rested in her general unease around strangers.

Pulling out her notebook, she forced herself to attend to the work at hand—preparing copy for newspaper advertisements inviting Christian authors to contact them. They'd tested several different advertisements in London and a few other key cities in the U.K., and she was beginning to get an idea of what worked for their target audience. Graham had been pleased with her marketing work. She scribbled down some ideas, but the situation with Mr. Sutton continued tugging at the edge of her thoughts.

A solitary lunch in her usual Belgrave Square spot allowed her time to revisit her thoughts on Mr. Sutton. Graham's calendar was filled with his appointments with authors. It was an ideal place for someone to find out which authors they were pursuing. Could she possibly have made a mistake? Maybe Graham told him to copy down something from the planner. If it turned out to be nothing, would Graham think her silly? Was it just her wild imagination, another flight of fancy, at play again? She thought of the way John Sinclair had readily accepted his parents' dismissal of her worthiness as his wife because of her overactive imagination. Would this ruin her chances of anything more than friendship with Graham?

She shook her head. It didn't matter. If there was even a possibility she was right about Mr. Sutton, she couldn't take a chance on not letting Graham know.

With resolve, she packed up her things and returned to work, more determined than ever to do what was right regardless of the outcome. But she did ask God to help Graham hear her out and understand that her heart was in the right place, regardless of whether or not Mr. Sutton had done anything wrong.

Margaret clenched and unclenched her fists as she handed Graham her advertisement concepts upon his return. He looked over the page and discussed some ideas for a couple of adjustments.

"Another excellent job, Miss Elliot." He handed the page back to her.

She reached for it with one hand while her other played with the edge of his desk. "I saw that your friend Mr. Sutton stopped by."

"Oh, yes." Graham grinned. "He left me a piece of my favorite Derbyshire pie from the diner we often ate at when I worked with him at Hall & Wright. I feel quite ashamed that I don't do the same for him, but I don't think it appropriate to stop by my old employer's office. Though he says I more than make up for it when he comes over to have a meal made by Cook at the house. Whenever she knows he's coming, she includes some of his favorite foods."

Margaret bit her lip and nodded as she considered how to turn the conversation back around. "I suppose . . . you must have told him to check your daily planner so he would know when you would be in your office."

Graham tilted his head and furrowed his brow. "What do you mean?"

Her heart raced, and she plunged ahead. "Only that I came by to say something to you, and he was looking through your planner and writing things down from it. I left and didn't say anything. I wasn't sure what to do."

Pushing his chair away from his desk, Graham leaned back and crossed his arms. "No . . . I've not asked Charles to get any information from my planner. That's . . . Are you sure that's what he was doing?"

"Well, I didn't see what he wrote, but he was slowly and carefully running a finger down what I know is your planner while he looked back and forth at a notebook that he was writing in. He was paying close attention, as one would do when copying down what they were reading. Then he left a few minutes later with the notebook he had been writing in."

Graham tapped his chin, then reached forward and opened up his planner, flipping to the correct week. He looked it over and flipped a few pages before meeting Margaret's eyes.

"What are you implying?"

Margaret swallowed and worked to find her voice. "I . . . I hope I'm wrong, but after talking to your mother—"

"My mother?"

"Yes, she mentioned that when your father died, there were people from inside Corbyn Steel, trusted men, who worked against your brother to try to take the company away. She wonders if someone close might be the source of one or both of the situations we're battling." There, she said it.

Graham blew out a breath. "Then why didn't she tell me this herself?"

"I don't know."

"Does she think Charles has something to do with all of this?" He waved his arm across the desk as if their problems were laid out before them.

"No. She didn't mention any names. I don't think she has any names in mind. She wanted to warn me about what could be happening."

He rubbed a hand over his face and mumbled. "It doesn't make sense."

"I know it seems like a wild idea, but I wouldn't feel right if I kept the information from you."

"What do you suppose I should do? Invite my friend over and accuse him of stealing my authors? And the situation we're in involves authors who are going with a different publishing house than either Corbyn or Hall & Wright. He works for Hall & Wright, so it would be nonsensical for him to steal authors from his own company." He tapped his fingers on the desk as he reasoned through his thoughts.

"I agree—nothing adds up." She'd wondered about these things herself while she waited for Graham to return.

"I'll get my mother and have her join us. Maybe she has some insight."

"Good idea." Margaret nodded, but inside, she wondered if Mrs. Corbyn would also think she'd taken her words too far.

When Mrs. Corbyn joined them, Graham and Margaret repeated their previous discussion about Mr. Sutton.

"Graham, I understand your hesitation to accuse or think badly of your friend, and I quite dislike the idea of believing such about Mr. Sutton. But I have seen men who I held in higher regard than him fall mightily because of their drive for money and power. You should listen to Margaret on this," Mrs. Corbyn said. "Margaret, you've had longer to think this through than we have and are more distanced from this situation. Do you have any suggestions for what we should do with this information?"

She had thought through several ideas and hoped they sounded as rational to Graham and Mrs. Corbyn as they had in her head. "Perhaps we can wait a week and see if any of the authors on your calendar are contacted by this publishing company that's been going after our clients. In the meantime, we can talk with Mrs. Brown and see what we can find out about this other company that she was involved with. She's the only person we have a solid relationship with who was in negotiations with them. In fact, we should discuss that with her whether or not Mr. Sutton has anything to do with it."

"That sounds like a wise way to handle the situation. You're saying we don't accuse Mr. Sutton unless we have more proof that he has done something wrong?" Mrs. Corbyn asked.

"I am," Margaret said.

Graham's fingers stopped moving, and he nodded. "We can talk with Mrs. Brown. I still don't like that you believe Charles has anything to do with this, and I seriously doubt he does, but I can see wisdom in waiting before asking him why he was looking at my planner."

"Wonderful. I will return to the reception desk, and you two can continue to plan how to carry this out."

After Mrs. Corbyn left, Graham stood and moved towards her. "I'm sorry, Margaret, for doubting you, and I'm still not convinced Charles is involved, but I'm glad you told me your concerns. I appreciate that you are looking out for the company, and Mother is correct in saying you have more disinterest in whether Charles is involved than I do, so I don't take your warning lightly."

As he drew near, her heart raced, but it wasn't for the same reason as when she'd first told him about Mr. Sutton. Did he feel any of the emotions she did when he looked into her eyes, or did this intense look merely mean he appreciated her as an associate and friend? As they watched each other, she internally said, *"Tell me what you're thinking. Please make the first move if you're interested in me."* She did not want to be the one to chase after him. That had never been her style, nor would she know how to pull it off. *What was his mum thinking?*

He shook his head. "I don't know what my mother was thinking in telling you her worries instead of me, though I understand you're both apprehensive for the company's sake."

Margaret's face heated, and she looked away. At least she'd only said the last part about his mother out loud.

Chapter Fifteen

"H. W. Press was the company name on all of the materials I was sent by the other publishing company I was speaking with," Mrs. Brown said after Bible study the following day.

She sat at the conference room table with Margaret and Graham. They explained some of their situation, not only regarding the loss of authors but also the accusation from Hall & Wright, and she was more than happy to take the time to discuss her experience with the competition.

"I see that you are sincere about your faith, and I've come to trust your company," Mrs. Brown told Graham and Margaret. "In the beginning, Mr. Holt—Eddie Holt, according to his business card—said many things about his company that were similar to what you said, Mr. Corbyn, about how your company was looking for Christian authors. He quoted some scripture, and I thought he was sincere. So when he began promising much more than your company—one hundred pounds instead of the seventy-five you offered as an advance, and seven and a half percent royalties only for the first three thousand books instead of the first five thousand before rising to ten percent . . . It seemed like an obvious choice until I really got to know the two of you and the others who've been coming to the Bible study and work here.

After discussing it with my husband, I decided I felt more confident working with your company."

"We appreciate your candidness with us about this, Mrs. Brown. Do you have an address for H. W. Press?"

"I do not. Only a post office box. I guess I assumed they were tied to Hall & Wright as a religious division and were located there. But since Hall & Wright sued you, I'm guessing that's not the case?"

"I don't think so. One of the other authors we lost had gone with H. W. Press, and when we sent that information to Hall & Wright, they did not claim them as a division. After our discussion with you, however, we will certainly have our solicitor verify that." Graham sat on the edge of his chair and managed to look both kind and in charge.

Mrs. Brown pulled a card out of her pocket. "Here is the card Mr. Holt gave me, if you want to copy the information."

Graham reached for the card, but Margaret held out her hand to him. "I'll write the information down." She flipped to a new page in her notebook, where she'd been keeping information for the legal case.

He handed her the card, and she copied it.

"What did Mr. Holt look like?" Graham asked. "In case we meet him, so we can be sure we are speaking with the same person you did."

"He had brown hair, and I think his eyes were brown. His facial features were rather nondescript, and he wasn't much taller than me— so maybe five and a half feet. His most significant characteristic is that he walks with a slight limp."

"Thank you. If you think of anything else related to this that might help, we would greatly appreciate it." Margaret smiled at Mrs. Brown. "Your confidence in us and your friendship mean a great deal. Not only do we want to do our best for you, but if someone is taking advantage of other authors and we can prevent that, we will."

Mrs. Brown touched Margaret's shoulder. "Thank you, dear. I will be praying for the company and for your success in getting to the bottom of this." She stood to leave. "Oh, I almost forgot. This was in my mail yesterday. It seems they're trying to get me back." She pulled out a flyer and handed it to Graham.

Margaret slid her chair closer to Graham's to better see the flyer from H. W. Press. It looked similar to one they'd mailed out to potential authors the week before. Scanning it, she saw some of the same wording and verses.

Standing, Margaret said, "I'll be right back. I want to show you something, Mrs. Brown." Minutes later, Margaret returned with their version of the flyer and her planner. "We mailed ours out"—she flipped back a week in her planner—"last Monday morning. It wouldn't have gone to you though. It went to potential new authors."

Graham caught her eye, and she wondered what he was thinking.

Mrs. Brown raised a brow. "Anyone in town would have received it the same day or the next at the latest, and H. W. Press would have had time to make something similar and send it out."

"True. Thank you for sharing this with us. Would you mind if we kept it? Perhaps we can discover something else from it if we look it over more thoroughly."

"Certainly. I'm glad I can be of some help. I do hope things turn around soon with all of this. Keep me updated."

"We will. Will we see you at Bible study tomorrow?" Margaret asked.

"Tomorrow morning, I'm taking my mother-in-law to the doctor's office, so I will miss it, but I'll be back Thursday unless God has different plans. Good day to you both."

Graham and Margaret said goodbye, and when Mrs. Brown was out of earshot, Margaret turned to Graham. "You had a look on your face when you saw the flyer. What are you thinking?"

The smile he'd pasted on his face faded into a frown. "I'm thinking that I showed Charles that very flyer two weeks ago."

"Oh . . . I'm sorry."

He shook his head. "You think you know someone."

"There's still a chance it's not him." Despite her internal protest, she reached out and touched his arm. The thought that her effort would please his mother flitted through her mind, though that's not why she did it.

"There is. I suppose we'll keep waiting and see."

Margaret examined the words she'd copied from the business card again.

H. W. Press
Eddie Holt
PO Box 256, Great Portland Street Post Office
London, E.1
Telephone: WELbeck 4697

It was in the Marylebone area of London and only a couple of miles from Belgravia. The phone number was tied to the same area of town as well. Graham said that wasn't where Charles lived. She wondered about this Eddie Holt person and whether he had any ties to Charles.

A tap on her door drew Margaret's eyes up. "Come in."

"I have a thought." Graham leaned against the doorframe. "I have an acquaintance who works for the Daily Express and also writes crime fiction—that's how I came to know him through Hall & Wright. He would likely help us dig into this if I promise him exclusive rights to the story if anything is uncovered."

"You don't think we should go to Scotland Yard?"

"We don't know that it's a real crime at this point. It may just be a series of coincidences."

"True. This is all so strange to me. Maybe your friend can point us in the right direction."

"I don't know that I would call him a friend, though we have always been on friendly terms, and I did help him get a solid contract with Hall & Wright. He's a good guy and wants to see good triumph."

Margaret chuckled. "Don't we all. Yeah, contact him and see what he has to say."

His head bobbed. "Okay. This is all new to me, too, and I feel a little lost. It's invaluable having you as a sounding board. Thank you."

A flutter filled her at his appreciation. He trusted her. She was able to have both a vivid imagination and show that she could think rationally in the present. It felt good to have him to acknowledge that. "You're welcome. I'm in too deep now to leave you to navigate this on your own."

He grinned. "I'm glad. I'll call him and be sure to have you with me when I meet with him . . . if you'd like."

"I would. Thanks."

"Good. I'll leave you to it."

"Victor Webb. Call me Vic." The brown-haired man before Margaret held out a hand.

"Nice to meet you, Mr. . . . Vic." She shook his hand and stepped back as he entered the conference room of their office.

"Graham told me the things that have been going on, and I have to agree with you—I don't think it's a coincidence." Vic had a subtle cockney accent that slipped out when he said the word *have*.

They gathered around the conference table and shared in detail what had happened with the loss of authors, the accusations of Hall & Wright, the information they gathered from the six authors, and what they'd learned from Mrs. Brown. Vic took down pages of notes and periodically circled things and drew arrows. When they were done, he tapped his pencil on the table as he flipped back through the pages.

Margaret glanced at Graham, who remained quiet while Vic looked over his notes.

"I'll pose as an author looking to be published and contact this Eddie Holt fellow. We'll see what I find out. Since I do write and have a couple of short stories that aren't under contract, I can show him those. I'll use an alias so he doesn't connect me to the Daily Express and get spooked."

"That could work to get you in the door," Graham said.

"You said you checked, and that number is unlisted?" Vic asked, and

Graham nodded. "I also have some connections with the GPO and Scotland Yard, who should be willing to help me find an address for this number. I've got a feeling this is going to be something big." Vic tapped the table with his pencil. "And I get exclusive rights to the story?"

"As far as I'm concerned and Corbyn Publishing is concerned, you do. I'll be praying for you."

"Sure. You talk to the big guy up there, and I'll talk to some guys down here. Maybe we'll figure something out."

"I . . . thank you for coming and being willing to help." Graham frowned, and Margaret imagined he felt the same way she did. What do you say to a comment like the one Vic just made?

"Well." Vic stood up and grabbed his things. "Word of warning. From now on, don't talk about our investigation on the phone. Whoever is behind this may be listening in on phone conversations. Be aware. We can communicate in person and by mail. After I walk out this door, I'll only contact you as Mr. West, and you can send all letters to Mr. West. If I call, I will announce myself as Mr. West."

Graham looked at Margaret and raised a brow before turning back to Vic. "I understand."

"Good. I'll see myself out. I'd like to move forward on this as soon as possible. If we're lucky, I'll have an appointment with Mr. Holt before the end of the day. Thank you for calling me, Graham. Good day, Miss Elliot."

Graham and Margaret stood as Vic left.

Margaret turned to Graham. "This is a step in the right direction, but he makes it sound a bit dangerous."

"Indeed."

"He's an interesting character, and he seems to know how to go about this sort of thing. What's next, boss? Is there anything else we can be doing in the meantime?" Margaret tried unsuccessfully to imitate Vic's accent.

Graham chuckled. "I think we'd better get caught up on some of our regular work. If we neglect the authors we do have and lose them, too, it won't matter if we find out more about who's behind all of the author stealing."

Chapter Sixteen

"**M**r. Webb . . . West, how may I help you today?" Margaret sat at the reception desk Thursday morning.

"Now, now, Miss Elliot. I told you to call me Vic. That takes care of the last name confusion."

"You did, sir. I mean, Vic."

He chuckled. "That's better. I thought your office was next to Graham's. Am I going to have to talk with him about how to treat you?"

"That won't be necessary, Vic. I'm just filling in for Mrs. Corbyn while she does some work at church."

"I suppose that's okay if she's off doing good deeds. Is Graham here? I've got some information for the two of you."

"I'm afraid he's out for most of the day trying to get caught up on some things. I can give the information to him."

"Sure." Vic pulled a notebook out of his pocket and put it on the desk. "Here. You can copy this down. It's the address for the phone number that was on Eddie Holt's card. My Scotland Yard contact came through. I haven't checked it out yet. You two might want to drive by and see what kind of place it is. Lots of shops in that area."

"Yes, we can do that." Margaret wrote the address down. "Thank you, Vic. We appreciate all of your help."

"No problem. I also called and left a message for Eddie. I'll let you know what happens with that."

"I'm sure Gra—Mr. Corbyn—will be happy with this news. Thank you again."

Vic raised an eyebrow, and one corner of his mouth followed. "Graham, is it? You two make quite the pair. I'll see you later, Miss Elliot. You take care." He set his hat on his head and turned to leave.

Margaret stood up. "But we're not—"

He glanced back. "Keep telling yourself that." With a wink, he turned and left.

Margaret huffed and dropped back to her seat, shaking her head. It was obvious to others, but was it obvious to Graham?

The address she'd just written caught her eye, and she wondered at what kind of place this Eddie Holt person worked. They'd searched the phone book and not found a listing for H. W. Press. Tapping her fingers on the desk, she recalled the London map at her desk and stepped away from the reception desk to retrieve it. She estimated it would take about twenty minutes to get there by bus, but a taxi could likely make it in ten. It looked like it was about two and a half miles.

Just before lunch, Mrs. Corbyn returned, and Margaret told her she was going to Marylebone. She also left a note for Graham with all she'd learned from Vic. Using her lunch break to help him might assist him in appreciating her as an asset both to the company and to himself.

"Are you sure you'll be okay? Why don't I have my driver take you? I can call him when he's back at his garage and have him return."

"Oh, no, ma'am. I'll be fine with a taxi."

"Well, I insist on paying then." Mrs. Corbyn pulled out a ten-shilling note.

"That's too much."

"Just take it. You can use the extra for lunch." Mrs. Corbyn took Margaret's hand and placed the note in it.

"Thank you, ma'am."

"Thank you for doing so much for Graham." Mrs. Corbyn's sly smile said what her words only implied.

Yes, part of Margaret was doing it to impress Graham, but her curiosity held just as much sway in her actions.

"You can drop me off here," Margaret told the taxi driver as he pulled onto the side street next to the address Vic had given her. When they drove past the front, she had read the words Crawford's Curios painted in elegant gold letters above the awning.

After paying for the taxi, she walked across the street to the side of the shop and peered in the windows. From the elegant old furniture she saw in the window, she guessed it was an antiques shop.

"Margaret," came a familiar voice at the same time as a hand wrapped around hers, pulling her to a standstill.

"Graham!" She turned wide-eyed to the voice.

He lifted a finger to his lips. "Shh."

Her eyes lingered on his lips as she whispered, "What are you doing here, and why do I have to be quiet?"

"Charles is entering this shop." He pointed to Crawford's Curios. "I just happened to be driving by and saw both of you. What are you doing here? Though I have my suspicions."

Margaret looked back at the road, and there his car sat against the curb near them. She'd been so focused on her inspection of the store, she'd not noticed him pull up.

"Did your mother give you the message?" She wondered if Mrs. Corbyn had known where he was and reached him while he was out.

He shook his head. "I've not spoken to her since I left this morning. I just finished my appointment at a café down the street. I saw Charles in front of the building and thought I'd pull over and see if I could figure out what he was doing. Imagine my surprise finding you already here." He tilted his head. "You're not meeting him here, are you?"

She analyzed his look. Was he insinuating that she was working with Charles against him?

"I had no idea he would be here. If anything, I imagined I might cross paths with our Mr. Holt. Not that I could be sure it was him, aside from Mrs. Brown's description and the limp. Who knows how many men in London have a limp?"

While she spoke, Graham tilted his hat low over his face, stepped away from her, and peered around to the front of the building. He shook his head and stepped back toward her.

Continuing her explanation, Margaret said, "I came because Mr. Webb stopped by the office while I was working at the reception desk for your mother. He brought the address that the phone number on Mr. Holt's business card is coming from but said he'd not had a chance to drive by and see what was in the building. I wanted to help you get a head start on it and came by during my lunch to see for myself."

Something on Graham's face shifted, and a crease between his brows formed. "You skipped your lunch and risked your life?"

"Surely Mr. Webb was making it sound more dangerous than it is." She smiled and relaxed now that he no longer seemed to doubt her intentions.

"I have no idea." He frowned and shifted his feet. "And your safety isn't worth the risk."

"Thank you for your concern." Now she took a turn walking nearer the corner of the building so she could see the activity in front. No sign of Charles. He could have come and gone while they spoke, but she'd been watching in case he passed in their direction. "Also, Mr. Webb said he called Mr. Holt's number and left a message but hasn't heard back. He'll let us know when he does."

Graham nodded at the information. "That's good."

He moved to the corner of the building and gazed toward the front door. His eyes grew large, and he strode back to her side while guiding her closer to the building and leaning casually against it with his back to the front and an arm propped against the wall to partially shield Margaret.

"Charles is walking this way. Look around me and watch in case he's with anyone or is holding anything that might give us insight."

She watched and did see Charles pass, though he was alone. He held a briefcase in one hand.

A breeze blew past them. Graham's signature lemon scent wafted across her and combined with the warmth of his body, causing her to momentarily forget what she was there for.

"Has he passed?"

"Oh . . . yes." She blinked and looked up at him. "No one was with him, and he carried a brown briefcase."

"Excellent work. He didn't have that when he entered." He rubbed his chin between his thumb and forefinger. "I may need to invite my friend Charles over."

"I'm curious to know what you have in mind, Graham."

"It's working hours, so I'm Mr. Corbyn." One side of Graham's mouth lifted. "But considering that you took your lunch to do this, I'll let it slide."

Margaret poked at his chest. "And considering I'm still technically on my lunch break and we are not at the office, Mr. Corbyn."

"Much better." His smile reached his eyes, and his gaze dropped to her lips. "Miss Elliot."

"I feel a little like Miss Marple. I can't stop thinking about what we'll do next or what mysteries we'll discover." She stared at Graham's desk, covered with items Vic brought for them to use as disguises.

"I daresay you're hardly like Miss Marple." Graham looked Margaret up and down as she sorted through the wigs.

Margaret stuck out her lower lip. "You don't think I can figure out a mystery?"

"More that I don't think your youth matches the elderly persona Mrs. Agatha Christie gives her."

His soft smile nearly made her heart stutter.

"Oh." She wanted to appear disinterested, but it was difficult to tear her eyes away from him when he looked at her like that.

"What about this one?" She held up a poodle-cut wig made with black hair.

Graham wrinkled his nose. "It's not exactly your style."

"That's the point, Sherlock." She threw a hand on her hip. "Vic brought these disguises so we won't look like ourselves when we follow Mr. Sutton."

"You're right. I suppose that's exactly what you need, but I much prefer the way your hair is styled to that." He pointed to the wig.

Margaret tilted her head and raised a brow. "Why, Mr. Corbyn, are you complimenting me on my appearance?" She immediately heated from her own forwardness, but when he bit back a smile, her awkwardness faded . . . a little.

"Yes, Miss Elliot, I am."

His frank admission made her want to fan her face, but she dared not betray her feelings any further in the moment. Her heart couldn't handle the silent admission.

"What about this for me?" He held up a man's brown wig and mustache-beard combination.

It was her turn to wrinkle her nose. "I much prefer you without a mustache and beard."

"Touché, my dear Miss Elliot."

My dear. Internally, she sighed. Was Graham merely teasing her, or was there more to those words?

He pulled out his pocket watch. "Charles should be here in an hour. We need to get everything into place. My driver plans to arrive just after Charles is expected, so you can take these things to the car then." He gathered up the items and added a pair of glasses, a worn tweed jacket, and a flat cap. They contrasted greatly from the elegant suit jackets and fedora he usually wore. After stuffing them into a basket, he handed it to her.

"That should do it for me. And as Charles won't have seen you today, you ought to be perfectly fine wearing this dress." He gestured to the one she wore. "The wig should be enough to throw him off with you."

"We'll see, I suppose."

He touched her arm. "If you don't feel comfortable doing this, I'll work out something else."

"Oh, no. I may be nervous, but I'm not missing out."

He chuckled. "Alright. I'll leave you to it and see you in a little over an hour."

"Got it, boss." Margaret tipped a pretend hat and gave her best shot at a cockney accent before leaving him and walking to her office.

The moment Charles passed from the reception desk to the hallway on his way to Graham's office, Mrs. Corbyn peeked into the closet where Margaret was hiding.

"He's here. I'll be praying all will go well."

With that, Margaret thanked her and met the driver at the car on the opposite side of the Corbyn office building.

Graham had invited Charles over with a promise of Victoria sponge cake from the tea shop nearby. He'd explained that it was repayment for all of the treats Charles had given him. Graham planned to join Charles on his way out with the excuse that he had to run to a shop across the street to pick up something for his mother. If everything worked out, he would double back and hop into the car with Margaret, and they would follow him to see if they could discover anything else.

Sitting in the back seat of the car, with the Corbyn's driver up front, Margaret nervously tapped her fingers on the seat. She'd donned her wig and had pulled Graham's items out of the basket so they were ready for him to put on the moment he hopped into the car. She opened the jar of spirit gum and painted it on the back of the mustache and beard in preparation.

"There they are," Mr. Simon, the driver, said softly.

Margaret turned to see Graham and Charles leaving the building and saying their goodbyes before separating. She followed Charles's direction so she'd know which way they should drive once Graham got to the car.

"Miss Elliot . . . Mr. Simon. Good to see you both."

Margaret glanced at Graham and gave him a smile and a quick nod before her eyes found Charles's location again. He was entering a bus.

"Follow that bus." Margaret reached over the back of the seat to point out the direction.

While Mr. Simon started the car and followed, Margaret helped Graham with his disguise. She painted the spirit gum on his chin and above his lip, then carefully attached the beard. Daring to look into his eyes, she found him watching her closely. As she pressed her hand against his face, her heart raced. She wished there might come a day when she could touch his face freely and it would be a natural part of their relationship.

The feel of his fingers over hers startled her, and she gasped. His hand held hers in place for only a few seconds, but it felt like hours before he lifted it.

With her own shaky hand, she reached down for the mustache and gently placed it above his mouth. His soft chuckle broke their silence.

"That tickles," Graham said.

Margaret joined him in laughter.

She slid back to allow him more space to put on his wig and don the tweed jacket. Her heart needed the space as well.

When he took off his tie and dress shirt, the sleeveless white vest underneath revealed his toned arms. *Does every part of him have to be so perfect?* He slipped on the tweed jacket directly over the vest for a more common look than she'd ever seen on him.

"These pants will have to do. I can't change them in the car." He waved a hand, motioning to their cramped quarters.

"Gray is a neutral color. Hopefully they won't stand out too much." Margaret took in the outfit and held up the used shoes he'd found for this disguise. Maybe they would offset the pants.

"You're looking the part yourself." He eyed her gray and white pinstriped shirt dress, biting back a smile.

The dress buttoned from top to bottom and had white piping around the collar, chest pockets, and cuffs of the three-quarter-length sleeves. She'd added a loose-fitting navy wool cardigan over it. The look was nothing like the more up-to-date styles she normally wore. Before leaving her home in Steventon, she and her mum had put hours into her wardrobe, purchasing the best fabrics they could afford and then using the latest patterns to turn them into creations rivaling those at the finest department stores. This ordinary dress didn't flatter her figure at all, but most importantly, it wasn't likely to draw attention.

She patted her wig, still adjusting to the lack of hair at her neck. "Thank you."

Taking a deep breath, she tried to relax. She didn't know if all of the tension was from being nervous about their plan or from his careful examination of her along with their close proximity. Even though he made her nervous, she couldn't tear her eyes away from his.

"There he is," Mr. Simon said as he pulled up to the curb behind the bus. "He's off the bus and walking into that pub."

Graham slipped on his fake glasses. "God, direct us in this," he said just as Charles walked into the pub. Graham opened the door, stepped onto the pavement, and held out a hand to Margaret.

He leaned into the open door of the car before closing it. "Mr. Simon, why don't you pull around and park on that side street?" He pointed to a street several shops away before shutting the door and tapping the top of the car.

When the car pulled away, he turned to Margaret. "Let's do this."

Upon entering the pub, Margaret was hit with the scent of ale mixed with something savory. The smell of the food should have been appetizing, but with how tight her nerves were strung, it held no appeal.

The space was dark, and the furniture looked well worn. Her eyes adjusted, and she recognized the back of Charles's head. He was seated in a booth across from a man with brown hair who appeared to have a stocky build. She glanced at Graham, and he nodded before guiding her to a booth on the opposite side.

"I'll order us something," Graham said once she was seated. He turned and stepped up to the bar.

While waiting for him to return, she scanned the room. There were only a few others there. Two men were at a table near where she sat, and another man was two booths away from where Charles sat. She honed in on Charles and the man he was with. They appeared to be in a deep discussion.

"I ordered you a lemonade," Graham said as he slid a bottle of lemonade towards her and set down his own ginger beer. He turned back and picked up several other items from the bar and returned to the table. "It's not much, but you can't go wrong with cheddar." He pointed to a plate of chunks of cheese and bread with a side of sliced pickles and apples. "If you'd like, I can get you a bag of crisps."

"No, I don't have much of an appetite, so this is perfect."

He nodded and angled his body so he could see the table with Charles better.

"I think that might be"—he leaned in—"Eddie. If he stands up and walks, we'll have a better idea."

"Hopefully they don't stay too long. We might look suspicious if we linger over lemonade." Margaret ran her fingers up and down the cold bottle. "That's the notebook he copied your planner information into." She noted the notebook Charles had laid on the table.

They watched as Charles slid a paper from inside it and handed it to the other man. The man cautiously scanned the bar, and Margaret shifted her own eyes to the bread and cheese plate. She steadied her hand as she reached for a piece of cheese.

Graham's expression tightened. "I left him in my office for a few moments while I stepped out with the excuse of"—his face reddened—"using the lavatory. I'd planted some false information that might give us more concrete evidence of his getting information from me."

Margaret frowned. He'd not told her about this part of his plan.

"It was a last-minute decision. I'll explain later. I—"

Charles stood up. He put on his hat and turned to leave.

Graham shifted his body away from Charles's view and lifted his drink while Margaret brought a large piece of bread to her mouth.

Once Charles had left the building, Graham spoke up. "Let's eat for a few minutes and see if the other man leaves. I'd sure like to know if he has a limp."

Chewing the bread, Margaret nodded.

Several minutes after Charles had left, his companion walked past— with a limp. Margaret's eyes found Graham's, and he lifted a brow.

Chapter Seventeen

Riding back to the office in the back of the car, Margaret's heart pounded and her mind raced. What was Charles up to with this Mr. Holt?

Graham worked at taking off his disguise, and Margaret took off her wig and cardigan. She pulled a compact mirror from her purse and set about smoothing the small bun she'd made with her hair under the wig.

When Graham pulled off his wig, it left his hair in disarray. Margaret giggled and handed him a comb.

"How's that?" he said after combing through it.

"Much better. It's just that"—she reached towards his chin—"some of the spirit gum is stuck to your chin."

He touched the area she was reaching for with mineral oil and rubbed at it. "Did I get it?"

"Not all of it."

He rubbed again to the left, and she shook her head.

"Here." She dabbed some oil on her finger and reached again. "May I?"

He nodded, and she rubbed the glue off of the spot. "Much better." At his penetrating gaze, her hand froze.

Like on the ride over, he covered her hand with his. "Yes, much better."

He pulled her hand down but didn't release it. Instead, his thumb caressed the back of her hand.

For the rest of the drive, they sat silently in the backseat, hand-in-hand. She wondered what this meant for their future.

"George, my contact at Scotland Yard has requested that the two of you step back from this. It's not safe." Vic stood with Graham and Margaret in the conference room of Corbyn Publishing. He'd arrived just before they returned from following Charles and had been in the middle of leaving them a long note when they stepped into the office.

Margaret held a picture of Eddie Holt that Vic had brought. He was the very man they'd seen meeting with Charles at the pub. Vic had met with Eddie under his alias author persona, then followed him and taken a picture.

"George says this guy has ties to the Morton crime family, and you do not want to get involved with the Morton family," Vic told them.

"Charles is mixed up with a mob family?" Graham asked incredulously, color draining from his face.

"He is. Whether he knows it or not is another question."

Margaret tensed at the news. "Even in Steventon, I've heard of the Morton family." She recalled reading in her local newspaper about the crimes the family was committing in the London area—fraud, violence, and racketeering—though she wasn't sure what racketeering involved.

"My word! I can't imagine how Charles got himself pulled into this mess." Graham paced the room.

Vic crossed his arms. "Things like this used to shock me, but not anymore. I've seen a lot on the crime beat."

Margaret wasn't sure what to make of it all. "I can't believe we were so near a mobster."

"Margaret." Graham's gaze shifted to her. His face had become stony. "I sincerely apologize. I never intended to put you in danger. I only meant to get to the bottom of who was sabotaging our company. I should be keeping you safe."

"I went willingly, and I'm okay. None of us knew." She touched his sleeve.

"That may be true, but . . ." His voice trailed off, and he rubbed a hand over his face. "I'm truly sorry." He placed a hand over hers but removed it almost as quickly as it landed there.

"Wonderful. Everyone is sorry. Now . . . Scotland Yard is taking this seriously. George will be in contact with you. His last name is Sanderlin."

Margaret picked up her notepad and pen and wrote down his name.

"Thank you, Mr. . . . Vic. We wouldn't have any idea this was happening without you."

"No problem. Graham's a good man. I want him to succeed. With George's help, you'll get things figured out. Keep this picture. You might need it. I developed another I left with George." He picked his hat up from the table, set it on his head, and tipped it. "I'll be in touch to make sure things are coming together."

Graham looked dazed as he stepped forward. "I'll walk you out, Vic."

Margaret retrieved the picture and her notepad and stood outside of Graham's office. "What are your thoughts?" she asked the moment he returned.

"My thought is that I need to get you and Mother to a safe place. A man connected to the Morton family comes to the office regularly. I've locked the door and informed the others working today that there is concern for our safety. I've asked everyone to leave."

Minutes later, Graham, Margaret, and Mrs. Corbyn stood in the reception area discussing the situation when the Corbyns' driver, Mr. Simon, knocked on the door. Graham put him in charge of seeing that everyone left safely and no one entered.

"Mother and Margaret, please pack whatever you'll need at home. Mr. Simon will drive you home once you're ready." He turned to Mr. Simon. "Thank you for keeping them safe."

Without giving Margaret a passing glance, he walked by and reached for the handle of the door.

Margaret trailed behind him. "Where are you going?"

"To my brother's office to call Officer Sanderlin. Before, I didn't take Vic too seriously about the wiretapping, but now I am. Lock the door behind me. Don't open up for anyone who doesn't belong." He had the same stony look she'd seen on him just before Vic left.

She held up her notepad. "Why don't I go with you, and if there is any important information, I can write it down?"

He pressed his lips together and studied her before answering. "Fine. Follow me and don't discuss this with anyone. I'll explain things to my brother later."

They took the elevator to the top floor. Graham spoke with the Corbyn Steel receptionist, then he led Margaret to an office. It had no personal touches, only furniture.

"Is this someone's office?" she asked.

"It was my brother's, but when Father died and people questioned his ability to lead the company, Mother urged him to move to my father's office. At one time, it was my office. After returning from the army, I occasionally came in to help with things, or Mother did, and we used this office. I've not worked from here since I started my company."

In front of the desk, he pulled out a guest seat for her and walked around to sit in the desk chair. He slid the phone closer, opened a drawer, and tugged out a telephone book. After flipping through the pages and finding the number for Scotland Yard, he picked up the receiver.

"Wait." Margaret touched his hand. "Can we pray first?"

His stony face softened. "You're right. Thanks for the reminder. I'll pray." He bowed his head. "God, I've got so much going through my mind right now. Please settle my thoughts and give me wisdom and clarity. And I pray for your protection for my family, Margaret, and everyone affected by this. Show me what to do. In Jesus' name. Amen."

Margaret smiled at him but said, "Don't forget, you're not in this by yourself. I'm here, if I can do anything. And I think I can safely say your mother feels the same."

"You're right. I'll keep that in mind."

This time, he reached for the phone and dialed a number. "Yes, this is Graham Corbyn, and I'm calling for George Sanderlin." He listened before answering, "Thank you."

He covered the receiver. "They're getting him."

"Yes, hello, Officer Sanderlin . . . He did, but I had too many questions to wait."

Margaret listened with pen in hand for him to repeat important information during the conversation, but none came. Just a lot of "Mmhmm," "Yes," and "No, sir." Then he hung up.

Graham folded his hands on his desk but didn't make eye contact.

"What is it? What did he say?"

He tapped his thumbs against each other and finally looked up. "He's sending a plainclothes female officer to pose as my secretary at the front desk. She'll know what to look for and do if anyone unexpected comes in who might be connected to the Morton family or if trouble arises."

"That's wonderful. It will get your mum away from potential danger."

His eyes flitted to the door before finding hers. "I'd like for you to stay home as well . . . for at least a week. I'm not sure how long it will take for them to figure things out, but I don't want to put you at risk."

"Stay home?" She frowned. "Surely if there was a risk here at the office, it would have presented itself by now."

"Not necessarily. And once Scotland Yard moves on this, the Mortons may realize we had something to do with it."

Maybe there was some sense in what he was saying. "Okay, but can I do work from home?"

"Likely."

Why was he being so vague?

"Let's head down to the office so you can gather your things."

Minutes later, she followed him into his office with more questions.

He looked down at the desk, shuffled some papers around, and let out a slow breath. "Looks like Charles took the bait."

"How do you know?" Margaret asked.

"Because the fake contract I left out is missing. I completely forgot to tell Officer Sanderlin about my setup."

"What information was on the contract? Will it lead back to a real person?"

"I put down an alias and a PO box that I opened just for this. I'll close it when it's no longer needed."

"Do you think"—Margaret tried to put her thoughts into words—"What if the mob traces it back to you?"

"Good point. I need to call Officer Sanderlin back anyway once I return from taking you home. Why don't you pack up things from your office that you might need for a week or so of being absent. I'll take you home, call Officer Sanderlin, then return to meet the new secretary."

She didn't want to let him return to a potentially dangerous situation, but neither did she want to add to his worry. Standing, she said, "I'll be praying for you and this situation."

"Thank you."

Tension still etched his face in the lines on his brow and his rigid jaw, but she hoped that knowing she was praying gave him some hope.

Hurrying to her office, she surveyed her desk and decided on the items she might need over the next couple of weeks. She had a list of the authors they had contracts with and their addresses as well as the authors they were still pursuing. Those lists were of primary importance. Graham had come to depend on her for corresponding with the authors and engaging with them so those authors with contracts felt taken care of and those they were pursuing knew they were more than just a number.

She wanted to take home everything necessary to keep things running as smoothly as possible so they wouldn't lose their momentum. Perhaps now, with the law behind them, they could put the Hall & Wright lawsuit behind them and move forward with their growth.

Mrs. Corbyn was distraught about the possible danger her son was in. When Margaret arrived at the Belgravia home, she joined her in the parlor and filled her in on everything they'd discovered from Vic, Officer Sanderlin, and the details of what happened when they followed Charles. Mrs. Corbyn repeatedly asked her the same questions until Margaret suggested they get out their Bibles to read and pray.

That was how Graham found them when he returned home at the end of the day.

"Margaret and Mother, I'd like you and Katie to stay at my brother's for now. I'm coming up with a long-term plan and will let you know what that is soon. I still have some phone calls to make," Graham announced. "You should go ahead and pack your suitcases."

Katie had not returned from work yet, and Margaret dreaded telling her the shocking news. Only that morning, they'd been laughing about the disguises as if the situation was nothing more than a small-time attempt to steal authors—not a part of the mob machine.

Mrs. Corbyn looked at Margaret before turning back to Graham. "If you think it's necessary for us to leave, then that's what we'll do, but should we be worried we are bringing our problems to your brother's house?"

"After speaking with Officer Sanderlin, I think James and his family will be fine . . . for now."

"I will pack then. I certainly don't mind spending extra time with my other son and grandchildren."

"Thank you, Mother."

Margaret was pleased he was taking this seriously but apprehensive about possible long-term implications. "You're coming with us?"

"No, I'll be staying here. Officer Sanderlin says we must keep things as ordinary as possible."

"If it's not safe for us, how is it safe for you?" Mrs. Corbyn said with a wobbly voice.

"Scotland Yard will have plainclothesmen patrol the area. I've also spoken with Jones, and he plans to stay on at the house."

"Oh, dear. What will we do about Miss Hoffman and Cook?" Mrs. Corbyn laid a hand over her heart.

"They can go with you to James's home. He has enough room, and with the added guests, I'm sure their staff would appreciate the help."

"But then you'll have no one to cook for you." His mother continued to press.

"I'm a grown man. I'll have to make do. I'll be in my study making calls if you ladies need me. Let's have dinner at our regular time and leave an hour after."

"That only gives us an hour and a half altogether to pack," Mrs. Corbyn said.

"It does. If you discover you're missing something later, I'll gladly bring it to you." Graham turned to Margaret. "Jones will go to the mews house with you while you pack. I'd rather you not be alone."

She wanted to argue, but the steely look on his face kept her response contained. Instead, she nodded, and he turned away.

Once arriving at the mews house, she rushed to get a suitcase out. She began filling it and soon questioned if she'd need her other one. He'd mentioned a long-term solution. How long might it take for this situation to resolve?

She finally settled on packing for a week in one suitcase, and if she needed more, she'd ask Graham for help.

Just as she finished packing, Katie arrived.

"What are you doing, and why is Jones in our parlor?"

"It's a long story, and I'll give you more details over dinner. But right now, I need you to pack a week's worth of clothes. We're leaving to stay with Graham's brother for the night."

Katie looked around the room. "Is there a problem with this place? Can we not stay in the main house with Mrs. Corbyn?"

"No, it's—"

"Is this related to what you and Mr. Corbyn did with the disguises today?"

She might as well tell Katie the worst of it and get it over with. "It is, and we may not be safe here. Graham's friend Charles is involved with the Morton crime family."

Katie's eyes went wide. "I don't think I heard you correctly. The Morton crime family? As in mobsters?"

"The very same."

Katie's face paled, and it reminded Margaret of Graham's earlier in the day.

She pulled her friend into a hug, and with more confidence than she felt, she softly said, "We're going to be okay. Graham has a Scotland Yard officer working on the case, and he is already helping to keep us protected. We'll be taking every precaution. And what's more, we have God with us always."

Chapter Eighteen

J ames Corbyn was thirteen years older than Graham and had a wife and four children—all teenagers. He was a kind man but much more regimented than his brother. Margaret wondered if taking over a company as large as Corbyn Steel at the age of thirty had made him that way. Nevertheless, he welcomed Margaret and Katie into his home readily, and his wife Edith seemed more than happy to have three more adults around.

Their home was just as palatial as Mrs. Corbyn's Belgravia home but in the nearby Mayfair neighborhood. There were rooms to spare for their guests and the additional staff.

They provided Margaret a corner of the library to continue with her work for Corbyn Publishing. On her first day there, she doubled down on writing to both the contracted authors and their potential new ones. She was determined that Corbyn Publishing would continue its business even more effectively than before.

She hoped that Graham would have a chance to come check on them, but as the day wore on, it seemed unlikely. At five thirty, the phone rang, and the butler told Margaret it was for her.

"I'm at the Corbyn Steel Office," Graham said. "Officer Sanderlin has asked me not to visit you at James's home for now. They don't want to risk my leading anyone there and exposing you to harm. In the future when I call, remember not to speak of the case unless I tell you I am somewhere safe. Both the home and office may be compromised. And Margaret, that includes not asking me about work you can do. It might call attention to your not working in the office if anyone is listening in. Instead, we can communicate through letters throughout the day, or if something is urgent, you can call Corbyn Steel and ask the receptionist there to have me call. I have spoken to my brother about it."

"But you are at risk in that office and in your home." Margaret fiddled with the phone cord as images of Mr. Holt with his limp following Graham flashed before her eyes.

"Please don't worry about me. I'm taking precautions."

"I hope so."

Margaret then recounted the things she'd done for the company throughout the day, and Graham praised her for her diligence.

"How are things with the case? Any news?" Margaret was anxious to hear it was nearing a close. "Now that they know the connection between Mr. Holt and Mr. Sutton, surely things will move more quickly."

"I hope so, but it appears there is still much to be done. They've asked me to invite Charles over to see pictures I've taken with a new camera."

"What new camera? I didn't know you were interested in photography."

"I wasn't, but they sent a courier over with a camera for me to take photos with. I went outside and tested it with pictures of random streetscapes and things in the office, then took it to the place they recommended for developing."

"Why would they give you a camera?"

He chuckled. "I'm getting there. I'm to show him my pictures, and they hope to lift his fingerprints from the photos. They are also in the process of getting Hall & Wright's list of authors I was not supposed to contact. They are hopeful that they will find his fingerprints on it. I can tell you from working there that his fingerprints shouldn't be on it."

"That sounds like it could be helpful for the case."

"It would be, but it may not be possible with as many people who touched it when it was in question."

"I will pray about that. I'll be praying for you too. You have me quite worried."

"I appreciate it. It's difficult to keep on as if everything is fine when so much is at stake. The new secretary from Scotland Yard may be useful in other ways. She is to flirt with Charles and see if she can get him to ask her out. This might give us additional opportunities to get information."

"Good idea. What's her name? I'll be praying for her too."

"It's Miss Ivy Green."

"Ivy Green? Is that her real name?" Margaret held back a chuckle.

"You know, I can't say." He chuckled on the other end of the line.

"Well . . . it does seem like things are moving forward. That's good news."

Silence met her on the other end of the line.

"Graham. It is good news, isn't it?"

"Yes . . . it is."

"I'm not convinced, but thank you for staying and doing what is right to bring justice about. You are a good and godly man. I will be praying for you constantly. As for Corbyn Publishing, I will do all I can to keep things running smoothly from here. I'll mail out the letters to the authors as planned. Can we talk each morning to go over the day's plan and then in the evening to review?"

"I thought I was your boss, yet here you are holding things together."

"I'm doing what's necessary. We're going to come out of this better than before." She was intent on keeping a positive and upbeat attitude with him. It had to be hard for him to be separated from his employees and family and not have any assurances of the outcome for his business.

She had hoped he would bring up their hand-holding the previous day. So much had happened from the moment they returned to the office. Had he thought about it? At the time, she was sure it was a promise of something more in their relationship. She'd not mentioned it to Katie in hopes she would have some answers herself first.

"Margaret."

"Yes?"

"Thank you. I don't know how things will turn out, but I do appreciate it."

"You're always welcome, Graham."

The rest of the week followed the same pattern. She stayed at James and Edith's home for work while Katie left for her job at Selfridges. Graham called in the morning and late afternoon from his brother's office. Those were her favorite times of day. She wished he could come and visit but understood the dangers it posed. It was for the family's safety. Occasionally, Frances stopped by, which added some variety to the days. Frances was still reviewing and editing books for the company, and Margaret was glad another employee could continue working.

For lunch, Margaret discovered Berkley Square two blocks from the Mayfair home. It was not as quiet as Belgrave Square, but it was a nice reprieve from being inside most of the day.

Her first several days in the home flew by as she adjusted to a new place and working away from the office. At night, she and Katie sat in the parlor with the family after dinner. Their eldest twin girls were not present. She learned that they were seventeen and had recently left for finishing school in Switzerland. Their remaining son and daughter contented themselves playing board games while the adults chatted.

"Oh, look," Mrs. Corbyn announced. "Graham sent me a letter. It's rather thick." She opened the envelope, pulled out the letter, and held up a stack of photographs. "How wonderful. He mentioned he'd been taking pictures with a new camera." She flipped through them, stopping and laughing as she went. "Look." She held one up for everyone to see of a squirrel perched in a tree. Margaret could just imagine it overlooking her spot in Belgrave Garden. "There are pictures from around the office too. This one is labeled Miss Green. She's the new secretary." She turned it so the others could see, and Margaret caught a glimpse. She saw enough to know that Miss Green was a young woman with dark hair. When Mrs. Corbyn was done, she passed the pictures to Margaret, who was sitting next to her.

"Thank you." As she flipped through the photos, she, too, chuckled to see what intrigued Graham enough to warrant a picture. When she got to the photo of Miss Green, it unsettled her. She was a nice-looking young woman with a very pleasant smile, likely closer in age to Graham than she was. The thought of her smiling up at Graham as she posed for the picture had Margaret analyzing her for any possible flaw. Were her eyes too close together? Maybe it was worth the risk for Margaret to go back to work in the office after all. She rubbed her chest to relieve the tightness inside.

Friday, Graham called at eight thirty on the dot, and Margaret was anxiously standing by when the family's butler handed her the library phone.

"Good morning, Graham. How are you today?" She moved to the desk chair and readied her notepad.

"Good morning to you too. I'm at Corbyn Steel."

She knew that meant it was safe to talk freely.

He continued. "The news I have isn't good."

"What do you mean? Are you okay?"

"I am, but Scotland Yard believes this case will take weeks or months."

"I thought they were making headway."

"They are. They were able to match Charles's prints to the ones found on the Hall & Wright author list."

"That's good, right?"

"It is. They've even found his prints in my planner. And with your testimony of him copying information from my planner, and more recently, Mr. Holt sending a letter to the fake author on the fake contract I left for Charles, they have almost everything they need to put him away. But they don't want to move in on him until they get more on the Morton family. That could take some time."

"Oh." Months. He'd said it could take months. The full weight of it began to sink in. "Katie and I should look for a place to stay. We can't stay here with your brother's family that long, though I appreciate his hospitality. Maybe Mrs. Fletcher still has the room available where we stayed before."

"Actually, I've spoken with your mother and brother, and they would like you to come back home to live. At least until this whole thing wraps up."

"Home?" Internally, she deflated. "That will make it hard to keep up with things for Corbyn Publishing. It will be long distance for you to call me, and even mail would be inefficient with the longer delay."

"That's another thing. I've been praying about it and thinking things over, and I've decided that for now, we need to stop pursuing new authors. We can keep the authors we have contracts with, and I will keep working with them. Frances can edit their books. I know several excellent cover designers who have their own offices, so I don't believe that will be an issue, and I can have the printing equipment moved to a different location."

"So you won't need me?" She sank into the desk chair.

"You can keep sending encouragement letters to our contracted authors. I'll pay you another month's wages, and after that, a set fee for each letter you write. If you need other work, I have contacts with a number of publications you can write for. But if you need to get a full-time job elsewhere, I'll understand."

"I see." Not that she wanted to see or understand any of what he'd just said. She looked at her work list from the day before, and everything she'd done seemed meaningless.

"Your mother spoke with Katie's mother , and she is aware of the changes, though I know Katie will need to make up her own mind and so will you. Neither of you have to leave, but your families would prefer for you to be home for now."

"Home. I don't have a home at present. I'll be imposing on my brother's family. That's why I left in the first place."

"I'm sorry. None of this is easy."

It wasn't, and why wouldn't he talk to her about the hand-holding? If it didn't mean enough to him for him to bring it up, then she wasn't going to mention it. But it would be forever branded in her memory.

"No, it isn't." She wanted to get off the phone as quickly as possible. "So I suppose you don't have anything you need me to do?"

"I don't. This will give you time to figure out what you want to do."

"Okay. Thank you, Graham. Goodbye." She hung up before he could respond. She couldn't bear to hear another word from him. She'd never wanted to scream so much in her life. Where was this coming from? It wasn't like her to lose control of her emotions so quickly. She'd always been one to take her time and process how she felt.

She paced the room, wishing Katie wasn't at work. She needed to talk things over with her.

God, what is going on? I thought I was following where you led me— both in work and in considering a relationship with Graham.

She paced some more. She could stay in London and try to get a job with another publishing company. Maybe Mrs. Fletcher had a spare room. But did she want to stay in London, knowing Graham was nearby? He was pushing her out of his life. At least, it felt that way.

As for Katie, she doubted she'd want to stay if Margaret left. She'd not had a specific reason for coming to London like Margaret had. Katie wanted a grand adventure. It had been one—but too short-lived.

Recalling Jeremiah 12:1, Margaret whispered, "Righteous art thou, O Lord, when I complain to thee; yet I would plead my case before thee. Why does the way of the wicked prosper? Why do all who are treacherous thrive?"

Chapter Nineteen

"I can't believe you waited all this time to tell me Graham held your hand." Katie threw a dress into her suitcase before joining Margaret on the end of her bed.

One week had passed, and Margaret's brother was scheduled to come to London the following day to pick them up and return them to Steventon. As Margaret had guessed, Katie wanted to return with her and had given Selfridges a week's notice.

"I'm sorry. When it first happened, I kept waiting for Graham to talk to me about it so I'd have something more concrete to say. But then we found out about the Morton family, and the next few days were busy with adjusting to a new situation and making plans. At first, I thought he was waiting until things were calmer to talk about it. Then I began to believe it was my imagination that it meant anything."

Katie shook her head and frowned.

"And now I don't know what to think. Please forgive me for not saying anything before."

"Best friends aren't supposed to keep things like holding hands with the man they like from one another."

"You're right. And it was more than just the hand-holding. From the car ride over to the pub and leading up to holding hands, there was an electricity between us. Each time our eyes connected, I saw my feelings reflected in the intensity of his eyes. And each time I touched his face to attach his beard and mustache, I could feel something explosive forming.

"From first meeting him, I've felt a connection. I told you about that, though I tried to convince myself it wouldn't work. But in that moment when he held my hand, I saw him as my other half. Everything about him seems perfectly matched to who I am, yet it's nearly two weeks later, and he's made no comment about it or done anything to acknowledge that line we crossed."

"Oh, Margaret. I'm truly sorry. He does seem so well suited to you. Maybe he will speak to you soon about it after all. Perhaps he thinks he's keeping you safe."

"I don't know, and I don't want to get my hopes up. It reminds me of what happened with John, and it makes me feel like my younger self, pining after a man who's not meant for me."

Footsteps passed their room in the hallway, and they stilled.

After a minute, Katie whispered, "Margaret, you know this doesn't compare to what happened with John. Graham hasn't made a verbal commitment to marry you, and the two of you are better suited than you ever seemed to be with John. Don't write Graham off yet."

Could she hold out hope and not end up brokenhearted in the process? Katie was right about not comparing the two romances. Even though Graham had never made any type of commitment to her, the loss of him in her life would be worse. She already felt the loss from the recent changes.

She rubbed her eyes, wiping the moisture that filled them. "I've gone from seeing him constantly throughout the day to talking only twice a day to only a few conversations. Soon I doubt we'll even speak on the phone." She reached for her chest. "I feel an ache in here. Like part of me is missing. I should never have let myself become so attached."

Katie wrapped her arms around her friend and softly prayed over her.

Three weeks and two days had passed since Margaret left London. She settled into a spot under a tree in her brother's yard. The tranquility of Steventon that she'd always loved before was wearing on her. She'd become used to the bustle of London. Though her brother's property had a number of lovely walks and an elegant garden, she compared them to her spot in the Belgrave Square garden and found them lacking. But perhaps it wasn't the garden itself she missed, but the idea that at any moment, Graham might drop by and join her. Those had been happy times.

They'd spoken on the phone twice in the three weeks, and he'd written to her three times. When she told him she worried about his safety, he'd said, "I have to see this through. This goes deeper than you realize. Yes, it affects the company, but people's lives are at stake." Without his presence, she felt like a woman starved of sustenance.

Her eyes shifted to the blank page in her writing journal. She'd had no new inspiration since returning to Steventon. Her creativity had dried up.

A cold October breeze swept past, and she buttoned up her cardigan before pulling her Bible closer. She returned to what she knew would sustain her—God and his Word. Even if she didn't feel God's presence, she knew he remained faithful and ever-present.

Not that she hadn't spent much of the past three weeks shaking her fists at God and arguing with him about her situation. Her anger with God lingered, but she didn't give up on working through it.

"God, I don't understand. I followed your lead to London. I had no plans to look for romance, but only to provide for myself while I wrote for your glory. It seemed you had lined everything up for me to work at Corbyn Publishing. So where did I go wrong? Why did I develop feelings for him?"

No one responded. She turned to the Psalms for a reminder that even David had difficulty understanding why God allowed such difficulties into his life. She would keep clinging to the Word of God until her heart was moved and lined up more with that of her Maker.

That evening, she sat on the window seat in her mum's room, catching up on the day. Her days had begun to run into one another as she helped her sister-in-law with the children and wandered the property.

"You haven't been yourself since you returned from London, dear. I think you need a purpose. If you're not ready to look for a job, why don't you go with me occasionally to sit with Mrs. Woodhouse?"

She lifted her eyes to her mother and recalled the older woman who had attended their church since she was a child. "What do you mean?"

"Her husband passed away while you lived in London, and it became apparent that she has dementia. He had been covering her decline, and his death seems to have made it much worse. She lives with her son's family, but it is difficult for them to manage her because she requires constant supervision. Before they realized the extent of her confusion, she wandered off twice, and neighbors found her. I help out so they can leave their home on occasion. It's hard for Mrs. Woodhouse to go out. It adds to her confusion."

"Poor Mrs. Woodhouse. She was always so kind. I have good memories of her teaching me and the other children in church."

"Yes. She was—is—a good woman. This is one way we can honor her in her old age."

"I'll be happy to help. I have no idea how to act around someone with dementia, so you'll need to guide me. I don't want to make things worse for her." Thinking of Mrs. Woodhouse's situation made her own seem petty. Perhaps that was her mother's plan.

Margaret went with her mother to stay with Mrs. Woodhouse three times before she felt comfortable going on her own. Mrs. Woodhouse's daughter-in-law kept her dressed and her hair styled as if she were going out, but the expression on her face had changed from the lively expression she'd always had in the past. Now her eyes were unfocused, and her gaze wandered rather than remaining on the person speaking. She still spoke, but it was infrequent and in choppy, sometimes incoherent sentences. She often repeated herself.

Today Margaret sat with her at the dining room table, putting together a child's puzzle. It portrayed a boy holding a net and chasing a butterfly while a girl stood nearby watching. It only had fifteen pieces, and Mrs. Woodhouse studied it as if it had five hundred. She worked studiously on it until something outside the window distracted her. A few minutes later, she looked down, saw the puzzle, and commented on it as if she'd just seen it for the first time. This happened several times. Margaret imagined they could have her work on the same puzzle indefinitely.

When Margaret noticed her becoming agitated, she began singing "Amazing Grace," and Mrs. Woodhouse stilled and smiled. A couple of times, she repeated a phrase from the song. Margaret followed with "All Things Bright and Beautiful," and Mrs. Woodhouse clapped at the end. She wondered if reading scripture might have the same calming effect and pulled out the Bible she'd brought. Turning to the book of John, she skipped to chapter two, hoping that the story of Jesus at the wedding in Cana might still be familiar to her. Whether it was or not, it was hard to tell, but it did hold Mrs. Woodhouse's attention.

When Margaret finished reading the passage, Mrs. Woodhouse smiled and patted her arm. "Love you," the woman said and nearly had Margaret in tears.

As she walked home afterwards, she silently spoke with God. *If something like that ever happens to me, God, I want to be as kindhearted as Mrs. Woodhouse.*

Margaret decided there was nothing like staying with a woman in the last stages of her life to help one examine their own life with new eyes. During her walk, she recalled the way she had snapped at Dorothy, her brother's wife, that morning. But that wasn't her only failure. What her mother hadn't said outright was that she'd been grumpy and snappy with everyone in the household.

That needed to change. Was she so heartbroken over a man who had never officially pursued her and a publishing career that never began that her hurt overflowed into her attitude? Regardless of whether she ever saw Graham again or achieved her goal of publishing a book, she was a representative of Christ. Maybe she'd been too busy telling God what she would do for him to listen to what he wanted her to hear.

God, I'm sorry. I know I have no right to act that way. The talents you gave me are to be used for your glory alone. I don't think I misinterpreted the call to go to London and work for Graham. Maybe it was preparing me for something in the future. Please help me to listen carefully when you tell me what to do next.

Over the next week, Margaret's spirits lifted. She was determined to stop looking at her own problems and use her time and talents to help others. Soon she would search for another job, but she could hold off a few more weeks and take this time to change her perspective and live out what God was showing her.

In the meantime, Dorothy introduced Margaret to the headmistress of her son's primary school, and Margaret volunteered to read to them. She was determined to find something age-appropriate. In the Willow-land series she'd been writing, Mary and Sam were ten. She resolved to write some stories that happened earlier in their lives, when they were seven—the same age as her nephew—so that they might appeal more to his class. The stories of the younger Mary and Sam were a hit, even without pictures. As a class project, their teacher had the children make drawings for Margaret to use with the stories. They were very rudimentary, but Margaret loved them.

Between her time with Mrs. Woodhouse, days reading to the children, and time spent writing again, Margaret's heart was mending. God was giving her the ability to view Graham more objectively. That included praying for him daily, and the longer the situation lasted, the more concerned she became for his safety. God was teaching her to trust him. If only she were faster at learning the lesson.

When Saturday arrived, the day Graham had been checking in with her, she believed she had her emotions under control and ready for his call. First, he asked about her week, and she was glad to tell him about the positive changes in her life. Though she was no longer trying to impress him, she didn't like him thinking she was wasting her life. That had never been the kind of person she was, and it embarrassed her to think that even for a short while, she'd allowed herself to drift along.

"Margaret, I do believe things will move more quickly now with the case. Miss Green worked her magic and has been dating Charles for a couple of weeks. She's managed to get some information that has been helpful. And I told Charles we had to cut the company down to the barebones because we lost authors. In a way, that is true."

"How did he respond?" Margaret was surprised to find not much more than a twinge of jealousy at his comments about the lovely Miss Green.

"He acted sorry and said he didn't realize we were getting off to such a bad start. He made some trite comments about it being a hard business to get into." There was a bite to Graham's voice that it didn't usually carry.

"It must have been hard not to comment on that when he is at the center of the hard time we're having."

"It was, but I bit my tongue. Hopefully things will wrap up soon, and we can move forward with our lives."

"What's been taking so long?"

"Scotland Yard wants to have enough proof to take down the key members of the Morton family. If they leave the head or some of the critical members, the family can pick back up where they left off."

"Makes sense. So are you planning to pick back up where Corbyn Publishing left off once this is over?"

"I'd like to. If you've moved on to other work, I completely understand."

"We'll see when all of this wraps up. I do need to find work soon, and I don't know where that might lead."

"I understand. I appreciated having you while I did, and you will be an asset to anyone who hires you."

Their conversation lasted a few more minutes before he told her goodbye. Once again, he'd failed to bring up a desire for anything more than friendship with her. If he made it clear that he wanted her in his life, she would return to London without hesitation. But continuing to work for the handsome and charming Mr. Corbyn would likely fill her life with more heartache if they were no more than colleagues and friends. For now, she could control her feelings, but seeing him in person every day without moving towards a romantic relationship would take extraordinary strength of character. It seemed beyond her ability. A twinge of pain shot through her chest at the thought of not being part of Corbyn Publishing. How strange that she'd gone from not believing she was meant for romance to only wanting it with him.

Chapter Twenty

S itting in the front of the church she'd grown up in and watching a man besides her father preach still felt strange. Something inside her expected her father to step up to the pulpit at any moment.

Margaret inhaled the smell of aged wood mixed with the honeyed aroma of the beeswax used to polish the pews and pulpit. It combined with the scent of rosewater worn by many of the older women. She sank into her pew at the comfort brought by the familiarity and pushed away the clouds of losing her father. Being here brought back sweet memories, and she preferred to dwell on those as she worshipped.

She listened as the minister preached on Psalm 62. It was a short psalm of David, and if she'd not read in the bulletin that he was preaching through the Psalms, she would have thought it an odd one to choose. He read through the entire passage before commenting on it. She had to hold back a gasp. It was as if God's words had been penned for her from the first verse, where David spoke of his soul waiting in silence for God when he was in distress because of being under attack. Then in verse ten, it said, "Put no confidence in extortion, set no vain hopes on robbery; if riches increase, set not your heart on them." Extortion . . . robbery . . . the Morton family. In verse eleven, it reminded her that power belongs to God.

"Thank you, God," she murmured under her breath. How could she ever doubt his provision for her when he perfectly met her in her need time and again?

She lifted her handkerchief to her eyes to dab at the building moisture and caught Katie watching her with lifted brow. It had been several days since she'd spoken to her friend. Perhaps Katie could join them for lunch after church.

The moment the final "Amen" was spoken, she turned to cross the aisle and speak with her friend, but before she could get there, a tall man with sandy brown hair stepped in front of Margaret.

Standing back, she watched him approach Katie and speak to her. Katie's eyes sparkled with happiness, and Margaret moved to better see the man's face. It was Owen Lloyd. He appeared as animated as Katie. Inwardly, she laughed and cheered for her friend. Katie had chatted about Owen dreamily for years, but he was six years older and had never treated Katie as more than a little neighborhood girl.

Margaret turned to speak with others and give her friend time with Owen. A few minutes later, Katie's father approached, and Owen said his goodbyes. In moved Margaret as she hooked her arm around Katie's.

"I see you had a friendly chat with Owen," she whispered in Katie's ear.

Katie's cheeks grew pink, and she nodded. "Come to lunch, and we'll talk after."

"Perfect. I was going to ask you the same."

"Papa." Katie turned to her father. "May Margaret join us for lunch?"

"Of course." His eyes shifted to Margaret. "You are always welcome in our home."

"Thank you, Mr. O'Neil." She squeezed her friend's arm and gave her a knowing look. Katie was on her way to love. It was written all over her face.

That afternoon, the girls hid away in Katie's room, catching up on their week. The first topic was Owen and how he'd been visiting O'Neil's department store, where Katie was working for her uncle. Katie had been using the opportunity to show off all she'd learned at Selfridges.

Margaret delighted in her friend's happiness at the possibility of something wonderful with a man she'd always admired.

Once she had sufficiently gushed over her friend's prospects, Margaret shared her news about God's revelation to her through the sermon, and they both marveled at God's goodness. Not wanting to take away from Katie's happiness about romance, she was less ready to share about her conversation with Graham, but Katie would be upset if she kept it from her. Reluctantly, she recounted what Graham had said and her own feelings.

"Oh, Margaret, I'm sorry." Katie hugged her. "Here I'm going on about my own happiness while you are suffering."

"Katie, it's not all that bad. I . . . well, I am sad over it, but God has given me a reminder that he is working on things in my life, though this particular thing may not work out how I'd hoped. But regardless of what is happening to me, I will always want to celebrate joys, small and large, with you. Please don't hold back your joys. I expect to be kept up-to-date on every wonderful thing Owen does."

"Margaret, you're the best friend a girl could ever have." Katie pulled Margaret into a hug. When they separated, Katie's eyes sparkled. "I can't help but think God has someone out there for you now that you are finally ready for romance again."

Margaret nodded and smiled, but inwardly, her heart screamed that she had no interest in any other man.

Margaret's time with Mrs. Woodhouse became a highlight of her week. Occasionally, Mrs. Woodhouse was more lucid and shared things from her past. Most of her stories included Mr. Woodhouse. Margaret had heard a little of how they met and fell in love. Those were the times when life gleamed in Mrs. Woodhouse's eyes and the unfocused stare disappeared. Hers was a life well lived and filled with love and romance.

Lately, everywhere Margaret went, it seemed she was hit with romance and couples in love. Walking through town one day, she spotted no fewer than three couples holding hands or arm-in-arm.

Today as she left Mrs. Woodhouse, a spark of a story idea popped into Margaret's head. She chuckled out loud, and a passing couple holding hands eyed her with curiosity. The story was a romance. Of all things! She'd never wanted to write romance before, and now with her jumbled feelings about Graham, writing a romance seemed like the worst idea she could imagine. And yet . . .

Upon her arrival home, she pulled out her writing journal, and ideas flowed faster than she could write them down. *God, where is all this coming from?* The answer he gave was more words for her pages. She couldn't stop herself from making the male main character look suspiciously like Graham. Her heart fluttered as she wrote about him. Maybe this was God's way of giving her closure.

If Graham did continue on with Corbyn Publishing after this case with the Morton family ended, she wondered if she would have them publish this book. She could imagine him reading through it and seeing himself.

Already an outline formed in her mind. She wanted to add a bit of mystery and maybe even danger. She'd keep the storyline far from what they'd experienced—definitely no mob family. But there could be something else. Maybe an art thief who created counterfeit art to pass off as priceless art. And a scene where the male and female main characters disguised themselves would have to be part of the story.

Margaret grinned, imagining Graham recognizing their own experience. But her chest tightened as the tension of those shared moments flooded her senses.

Rather than shut down the feelings, she embraced them and funneled her emotions onto the paper.

A knock on her door startled her, and her mother announced it was time for dinner. She obediently followed and joined her brother's family. Throughout the meal, she nodded and spoke when spoken to, but internally, her mind was spinning her story.

The moment she finished, she made her excuses to the family and told them she had some work to do. No one questioned her, and she hurried off to bury herself in the story.

Outside the window, the sky grew dark, but she didn't feel the least bit tired. When her mum came by and told her goodnight, she showed some concern over Margaret's withdrawal, but Margaret waved it off and was thankful when she didn't question and soon left her alone again.

Page flowed into page of writing until the words began to blur. Margaret could no longer hold her eyes open, so she laid down her pen, closed the journal, and stretched. She fanned through the pages she'd filled and laughed to herself. It was nowhere near finished, but somehow she'd gone from an idea to an outline to pages of prose in one day. *Thank you, God.*

When she finally crawled into bed and laid her head on the pillow, ideas still swirled in her head. She was tempted to hop up and write notes to use in the morning but instead asked God to help her let it go and sleep. Nevertheless, the thoughts persisted and kept her mind racing.

Groggily, Margaret woke to sunlight peeking through the drapes in her room. She'd slept, but it wasn't restful. Lingering images swirled in her head—pieces of the dreams she'd had. If she could recall them with clarity, she felt certain they would fit together with her story. Closing her eyes, she relaxed into the bed and enjoyed the last few minutes of rest. She had big plans for working on her book today.

"Good morning, God," she whispered when she finally opened her eyes.

Sitting up, she reached past her writing journal for her Bible and Bible journal and turned to Romans. In the office Bible study, they hadn't finished Romans. She could easily spend many more months mining it for the gems of truth it offered.

With care, she flipped open her Bible journal and found a blank page. "I consider that the sufferings of this present time are not worth comparing with the glory that is to be revealed to us. Romans 8:18."

God's Word touched her right where she needed it. She was determined to continue writing this story, and next week, she would begin looking for a secretarial job in the area. London no longer held the same appeal.

By Friday, she'd nearly completed her story. It lacked only an ending.

The rest effortlessly flowed as scene after scene filled her mind. Now she was stuck. She'd taken long walks in town to see if the romance all around sparked an idea. Nothing. She'd taken solitary walks through fields, allowing her thoughts to wander. Nothing.

Perhaps laying it aside for a time was the most practical option.

After reading at the primary school, she strolled through town and scanned the buildings, wondering if any of the offices she passed needed a secretary.

Though she'd planned to wait until the following week to look for a job, she'd given her mother permission to share it with her prayer group. Not only were the ladies in the group good about following through with prayer, but they would make sure word spread about her availability. They were careful not to spread gossip, but once given permission to share, they wasted no time.

Passing Steventon House, the home that Jane Austen's brother had built after tearing down the rectory in which Jane had been raised, it occurred to Margaret that she was more like the beloved Miss Austen than she'd thought after all—writing romance but never finding her own happily ever after.

As she approached the walkway to her brother's home, Arthur pulled his car into the driveway. Checking her watch, she noted the time was 1:20 and wondered why he'd left the bank he managed so early.

He didn't pull into the garage and instead stopped just outside of it and rushed into the house without looking Margaret's way. Seeing the tension on his face drove her to increase her pace to the front door.

She entered just in time to hear her mother say, "What on earth has you so upset, Arthur?"

It was the same question in Margaret's head as she rushed to the parlor.

Chapter Twenty-One

"He's been attacked," her brother said with a wild look on his face as he paced around the sitting room.

"Who's been attacked?" her mother asked.

Margaret froze as she waited for him to say who it was. She feared she already knew.

"Graham. Their driver found him unconscious on the mews street behind his house late last night."

She couldn't stop the gasp that escaped as she dropped to a sofa beside her mum. "Graham's been attacked?" She clutched her chest. "He's unconscious? Does he have any external injuries?"

"He's been in and out of consciousness since they found him. A doctor is treating him at home for cracked ribs, bruises, and a concussion."

"Was it the Morton family? Is it safe for him to be home if he was in the mews street?" Margaret wondered if the very thing he'd tried to protect her and the others from had happened to him.

"We don't know who did it yet. Maybe we will once he is awake and talking. They have plainclothesmen policing the area while they're there. As soon as he's able to get around, they'll take him somewhere else."

"Who is *they*?" Mrs. Elliot asked.

"James and Mrs. Corbyn."

"Oh, dear. It worries me that Lavinia is there if it's not safe," Mrs. Elliot said. "I thought she was out of town."

"She'd returned to James's home recently, and when Jones called with the news, she refused to stay away." Arthur shrugged. "Can you blame her? You'd do the same."

"I suppose." Mrs. Elliot squeezed her hands together. "Arthur, will you pray with us for your friend?"

He nodded. "I apologize. That should have been the first thing I thought of." He drew near his sister and mother, and they clasped hands while he prayed for his friend.

After he prayed, Dorothy returned from running errands, and they explained the situation to her. Arthur agreed it was likely that the Morton family had a hand in the attack. It was too coincidental considering what had been going on with the investigation.

Margaret listened as long as she could before excusing herself. It had been a strain holding her true emotions back in her family's presence, but what would they think if she wept as deeply as she wanted to? They didn't know how intense her feelings for him were. Until this moment, perhaps she didn't either. The thought that harm had come to him and she could lose him made her want to go back in time and refuse to leave him. She wanted to be there with him now. Not seeing for herself how bad he was had her fearing the worst.

Shutting her bedroom door, she crossed the room and dropped onto her bed. The first tears were already falling, and in the privacy of her room, she held nothing back. In the weeks since she'd returned, she'd tucked her feelings for Graham down deep, refusing to let them ruin her life. Now it all surfaced—longing, loving, and for all practical purposes, losing Graham.

Tears turned into sobs as she let it all out.

Eventually, her breathing slowed. Sitting up, she pulled at the drawer in her nightstand for a pen and paper. She wanted Graham to have a letter from her when he was awake. Maybe she would tell him exactly how much she cared—no, loved him. She started her letter, and her hand was so shaky that the words were illegible. It wouldn't do, so she laid the paper aside. Perhaps her time right now would be better spent praying.

She began pouring out her worries to God for his recovery and future safety. Her admission of love for him followed, and she gave it over to God. Her mind knew that he might not feel the same, and she would need God's help to manage her feelings if that were the case. The verse in I John came to mind—"But perfect love casts out fear." It fell in a section on abiding in God's love. God's love was perfect love. That was what she would hold on to.

"God, help me lean on you in this. Help me not worry about things I cannot change—whether it be Graham's recovery, safety, or him returning my love."

She felt prompted to open her Bible to 2 Corinthians 4. She skimmed through the chapter and read verses eight through ten out loud. "'We are afflicted in every way, but not crushed; perplexed, but not driven to despair; persecuted, but not forsaken; struck down, but not destroyed; always carrying in the body the death of Jesus, so that the life of Jesus may also be manifested in our bodies.'"

"Oh, God, let me . . . let him not despair or be crushed. Strengthen our resolve, whether it is together or individually. We are your vessels, created to glorify you."

With a sense of calm, she reached once more for the stationery in her drawer and began a new letter. She shared scripture and encouragement with him and told him she was praying. In this letter, she shared love, but instead of telling him of her love for him, she reminded him how much he was loved by God. For whatever reason, God was holding her back from telling of her own love. She would trust him in this.

Arthur made daily calls to check on his friend and shared the news with the family. Each day, Graham was awake more, but he wasn't talking more than a few words. He signaled that he was in pain. He did confirm it was the Morton family, but until he could speak more, they had no details. On Sunday, Margaret passed Arthur in the hallway while he was on the phone. He reached out and touched her shoulder to stop her.

Placing a hand over the receiver, he said, "Mrs. Corbyn would like to speak with you."

Margaret's heart raced at the thought of hearing firsthand how Graham fared.

"Hello. Mrs. Corbyn?"

"Yes, dear. It's so good to hear your voice. I've missed you immensely this past month. Though I'm glad you've been safely at your brother's."

"I've missed you too." And she had. She'd grown to love Mrs. Corbyn almost like a second mother. She was kind and generous and exuded the love of Christ in much the same way as her own mother. "How is Graham doing?"

"Graham has been clinging to your letter since we read it to him. Thank you for sending it so quickly. And I . . . I don't know if I should tell you this." There was a pause on the other end of the line. "Well, I'm going to anyway. Your name was the first word Graham spoke, and it was before we told him we had a letter from you. He's not been speaking much—only a few words here and there since he spoke your name."

Margaret had so many questions, but only one surfaced. "He spoke my name first?"

"He did. I know that nothing romantic has happened between you, but I still think he has feelings for you. And at present, that's all I will say on the matter."

When Mrs. Corbyn said nothing romantic had happened, the memory of his touch on Margaret's hand as they rode in the back of the car after disguising themselves seized her. The vision of his bright blue eyes staring into hers melted her heart as if it were happening again.

"Okay," Margaret replied softly, fearing her emotions might break though if she spoke any louder.

"He did get out that the attacker told him not to interfere with Morton family business."

"It was as I feared—an attack by the Morton family." Margaret's heart raced.

"Yes, so we hope to leave here soon, though wherever we go, we will still need protection."

"Of course. When do you think that will be?"

"I'm not sure. He still has great pain when he moves around. The doctor says it's likely from his cracked ribs and the bruising on his legs. He also has a concussion and his right hand is injured, so he's not to do any reading or writing during the time he is awake. If you receive a letter from him in my handwriting, that is why. And I promise not to add to his words. I won't tease you further."

"Thank you. I'm so sorry he's suffering like this."

"Me too."

After answering Mrs. Corbyn's questions about how she'd spent her time over the past month, they said their goodbyes and she hung up the phone.

"He spoke my name first," she whispered and shook her head as she leaned back against the hall table.

She couldn't wait to get Katie's thoughts on that and also to share her worries for Graham, so she picked up the phone and dialed the O'Neil home.

"Good afternoon. O'Neil residence."

"Ann," Margaret said upon hearing Katie's younger sister answer. "May I speak with Katie?"

A giggle came through the phone before she answered. "Oh . . . Katie's at Uncle Patrick's house." Another giggle. "She heard a certain Mr. Lloyd would be there." Ann lowered her voice to a whisper. "But you didn't hear it from me."

"Who are you talking to?" Katie screeched just before there was shuffling.

"Ow!" said Ann. "It's just Margaret."

"Margaret?" Katie said into the phone.

"Yes, she's telling the truth. It's me," Margaret replied.

"Thank goodness. Just a minute." Then a muffled, "Off you go, Ann."

"Well? Is what she said true?"

"It is. How about I come over, where little ears aren't present?"

"Perfect. I have some news too."

"I do love him, and I would go to him right now if they weren't preparing to take him away to somewhere safer," Margaret said as she reclined in the window seat in her bedroom.

"Where are they moving him? Can you go there?" Katie lay sprawled out on her tummy on Margaret's bed, feet crossed in the air.

"They've not said yet where they're taking him. But what do you think about Mrs. Corbyn continuing to push for something between us? Is she just imagining things since she's hopeful? Am I just imagining things?"

"There's only one way to find out. Confront him."

"Confront him? He's in terrible condition, and you make it sound like I'm to attack him verbally."

"Maybe that wasn't the right word to use. You're right—you can't just charge in and demand he tell you his feelings. You need something that will get his attention."

"Can't I just work my way back into his life gradually and see what happens?"

"Nothing. That's exactly what will happen if you use that tactic, and you know it. That's what happened before."

"That's not true. We almost kissed."

Katie moved to the window seat and laid a hand on her shoulder. "I remember you saying your hand lingered on his face and you stared into his eyes. That was bold for you."

"True."

"So, Margaret, are you going to go into his room and caress his face and stare into his eyes?" Katie's smile broke through.

Heat rose to Margaret's face at the thought, and she chuckled.

"Well?"

"Of course not. Next idea?"

Katie tapped her chin. "I don't know right now. We'll have to work on it."

"Okay, but I don't think we'll have long to work on it. They'll likely move him soon. Maybe we should work on a plan for your love life too."

They both giggled, and Katie assured her she'd be praying about Graham's situation. She also shared with Margaret about the visit to her uncle's home with his visitors and her thoughts on a certain man she'd been infatuated with.

On Tuesday, a letter came from Kingsdown, written by Mrs. Corbyn. They'd moved Graham to her friend's coastal cottage. Mrs. Corbyn invited them to come and visit to lift his spirits, but her news that the investigation still continued was disheartening.

A plan began forming in Margaret's mind, and she couldn't wait to see Graham.

<h1 style="text-align:center">Chapter Twenty-Two</h1>

Margaret fidgeted with her skirt in the backseat of her brother's car as they turned onto the coastal road in Kingsdown. She wore the new wool dress her mother had made. It was cut from a deep teal fabric that Katie insisted set off her complexion and coloring to its best advantage.

It had been a month since she'd seen Graham, and she wanted him to recall the way he'd felt the day before everything changed.

While Arthur parked the car, Mrs. Corbyn stepped out of the cottage and approached them.

"Welcome," she said the moment they exited. "I do need to warn you—I've not told Graham about your visit. I didn't want to get his hopes up in case anything went wrong."

"Oh no," Margaret said out loud, not meaning to. "Will he be unhappy at the surprise? What if he doesn't feel ready to see us?"

"I've been preparing him all day. I told him he needed to get cleaned up because a nurse was coming to check on him."

"*Is* a nurse coming?" questioned Arthur.

"Yes. I did hire a nurse to come by and check on him, so that wasn't a complete lie. Though I should warn you, he looks terrible. He has a black and blue eye, his right hand is bruised, and he limps both because of the injured ribs and the bruising on his leg. So prepare yourselves and try not to look shocked. I fear he *will* feel self-conscious if you do."

"Can you handle that, ladies?" Arthur asked his mother and Margaret.

"I've had to put on a strong front more than once raising you children," Mrs. Elliot said to her son.

Margaret nodded but quietly prayed that God would help her. She'd always struggled with hiding her emotions, and the idea of seeing him for the first time after a month already had her on edge. The visual reminder of the attack might push her over.

At the door, Mrs. Corbyn turned and said, "He's in the parlor. I'll lead the way and let him know he has visitors. I think this will be a happy surprise."

Margaret touched her sleeve. "I . . . I'd like to hold back and surprise him a few minutes after the rest of you enter."

Arthur raised a brow, and Mrs. Elliot exclaimed with a smile, "Do you have an interest in Graham, dear?"

She'd not thought this part through and regretted not telling her mother how she felt before today. "I do, Mum." She glanced at Mrs. Corbyn and saw the twinkle in her eye as she winked at Margaret.

Her mother pulled her close and whispered in her ear, "I wish you the best."

"Thank you," she whispered back, relieved at her mum's response.

As the others filed into the parlor, she heard Graham exclaim, "Arthur, you're here, and Mrs. Elliot!" His voice softened towards the end of his sentence, so she moved closer to the entrance to hear. "Sorry, it hurts to speak that loudly, but you caught me off guard."

"Good to see you too. You gave us quite a scare." It was her brother speaking. "Don't try to stand. We don't expect a ceremony."

She moved closer to the edge of the door so she could peek in at the scene. Graham sat on the sofa, and Arthur was moving to join him. Graham's gaze darted around the room, and she caught a glimpse of his bruised eye. She pulled away from the door as his gaze moved her direction.

"How is Margaret? You didn't bring her?"

"Do you miss your assistant?" Arthur asked.

Margaret's chest tensed as she listened for his answer.

"I do. But . . . she was much more than that." Graham coughed.

Margaret wanted to run to him right then but hesitated.

"What do you mean by that, friend?"

"I mean that—"

"Why don't we give you some privacy?" Mrs. Corbyn said. "I'll show Sarah around."

Mrs. Corbyn and Margaret's mother exited the parlor, and her mother squeezed her shoulder as they quietly moved past her.

"Is that acceptable?" Graham asked.

She caught what seemed to be the end of Graham's request of her brother and ached to know what he had said just before.

"It is, Graham, but I think you shouldn't wait."

"Why do you say that?"

"Because there is someone else who would like to speak to you." Arthur's voice rose.

She froze, and everything she'd practiced jumbled in her mind. Reaching into her dress pocket, she pulled out her lifeline and unfolded the pages. *God, help me. I want to be in your will.*

Stepping through the threshold into the parlor, she willed her shaking to calm, and she watched for the moment his eyes found hers.

It happened so quickly, but she saw the instant recognition lit his face. Her joy matched his, and she rushed forward to wrap him in an embrace. Halting before him, the bruises covering his body reminded her that an embrace might cause him pain.

"Margaret?" His voice held all the wonder she felt. He held out his left hand. "I need to touch you and assure myself you're real."

"I'm very real." She met his hand with her right, and when he squeezed hers, she felt certain her heart had just restarted.

He didn't let go as he examined her from head to toe. "You are a sight for a weary soul."

"Graham." All other words escaped her.

"I'll go get the luggage from the car." Arthur stood and slipped out of the room.

Graham's eyes locked back onto hers, and he tugged her to the spot

Arthur had just vacated next to him. The papers in her hand fell to her side, and all her focus shifted to Graham.

"You're here."

"I am."

"I've wanted to talk to you . . . to hear your voice. But Scotland Yard was concerned both for my life and yours. They worried you would be in danger if I contacted you."

"Why would they worry about me?" She hoped it was because she meant as much to him as he did to her.

He bit his lip before saying, "The timing of your arrival couldn't be better. Just before your family came, I received a call from Officer Sanderlin. He said Eddie, Billy Morton—who is the head of the crime family—and several others who are their key people have been arrested. They have evidence to keep them locked up for years."

"Graham, that's wonderful news. To think you risked your life to bring about this justice."

"I did what I had to, but I regret that your life and my family's were at risk too. Once the trials are over, I'll feel even better."

"Was there something else you wanted to say before you mentioned your phone call? You said Scotland Yard worried I would be in danger." Though she had her own things to say to him, she wanted to hear more of what he was thinking first.

"Margaret." His hand released hers and moved to her face. He looked at her with that same tenderness she'd replayed in her mind since the day of disguises.

"I've told you before what an amazing woman you are and how perfectly your qualities complement mine."

She nodded, recalling the times he'd told her.

"That day . . . the day we wore the disguises, I was so close to asking if I could court you," he continued so softly, she could barely hear him.

The intensity in his eyes nearly undid her. She'd waited so long for him to speak to her about this. "Why didn't you?"

"When we found out the Morton family was involved, I feared putting you at risk. Later, I spoke with Officer Sanderlin, and he told me that everyone I cared about was at risk. My brother and mother were obvious targets, and there's nothing I could do except keep them away, which I did. But you . . . I didn't want to bring you any nearer to danger." His hand slid down to her chin, and the strain on his face revealed the struggle he had talking.

"Shh. You don't have to talk. You're in pain."

He shook his head. "I hated being away from you. I missed you." His face inched closer to hers.

"I missed you too."

"Margaret, I wouldn't have felt comfortable telling you any of this if those men were still on the streets. I'm glad"—he winced—"today is the day we found out about the arrests. It's a gift from God."

She nodded, at a loss for words.

"What I have wanted to say since I last saw you is I . . . I love you. I thought I knew love when I was engaged before, but it wasn't the same. You strengthen my relationship with God and point me to him. It makes me love you more. You make me want to be a hero . . . even when it might cost my life." He held up his injured hand. "All of this was worth it to know I did the right thing, and I protected others." She could hardly hear him now. "I knew I was doing what would honor God, but I also wanted to be a man worthy of you."

"You are." Her voice was as soft as his. "Graham, you are, and I love you too."

A smile lit up his face, and his eyes closed momentarily. "I've longed to hear that from you."

"I want to hug you, but I'm scared I'll hurt you."

His eyes opened narrowly, but a smile still shined through. "I'll lead." Moving his good hand down, he slid it around her and pulled her towards him slowly. His forehead tilted down and met hers, the scent of lemon and neroli infusing the air between them.

"Thank you for being patient with me," he whispered into her ear before kissing her temple. "There were many reasons I waited to pursue you as long as I did." He kissed her cheek. "One of them was because someone didn't think she was meant for romance." He kissed the corner of her mouth, and her heart skipped a beat. "I'm saving the next kiss for when I ask you to marry me."

She gasped, and he pulled back to look into her eyes. "And I will ask you . . . soon. I hope you're prepared."

"Yes" was on her lips when she remembered the pages she'd written that lay beside her. "Actually, I have a proposal for you."

He lifted a brow. "I'd like to hear it."

She reached for the pages. "During my time away, I wrote a novel."

"Is it part of the Willowland Series?"

"No, it's a romance."

"That's quite interesting. I distinctly remember you saying on your first day of work that you don't write romance, and adding that you lacked experience. Did something else happen while you were away?" One side of his mouth rose.

"It did. I started seeing love everywhere and realized I was in love. The story practically wrote itself. It has similarities to our story."

"Oh? And how does it end?"

"The way every love story should. With a happily ever after."

"I like that."

"It's all in this proposal." She lifted the pages. "I'll read it to you, but I've also brought the manuscript in my luggage, which I'm happy to read to you too. I don't want you to strain your eyes while you're dealing with a concussion."

"Perhaps you're more like Miss Austen than you believe."

"She said she could never write serious romance. I believe mine is quite serious." She leaned in and kissed him on the cheek. "And also, I'm living my romance out."

"So you're not quite Miss Austen?"

"Exactly."

"Good. I'd much rather court Miss Elliot than Miss Austen."

"There will be no more 'Miss Elliot' coming from your lips."

"No?"

"No. Only Margaret from now on."

His eyes narrowed, and his smile twisted mischievously. "I hope to have another name for you in the future."

She arched her brow. "And what would that be, Graham?"

"You'll find out soon enough. But first, you must allow me to tell you how ardently I admire and love you."

Her whole body warmed at his words. "I think my heart can handle it, Mr. Darcy."

Chapter Twenty-Three

Three months later

Margaret's gaze drifted out the car window to the silhouette of Graham's face. They were on their way to Kingsdown as he drove them to Mrs. Price's cottage to meet his mother. The last time Margaret had been driven there, she'd been hopeful Graham would be receptive to her laying her heart out before him. Never would she have dreamed he would beat her to it or that the next three months would hold so much joy. This time as they approached the cottage, she was filled with a flood of happy memories of the day he told her he loved her.

Graham turned on his recently installed car radio and twisted the knob to search for music when they heard an announcement on the BBC channel. He glanced at Margaret, a knowing look passing between them, and she nodded.

"Breaking news. Mob chief Billy Morton has been sentenced along with a number of others from the organization." The announcer spoke for several minutes, detailing the prison sentences and speculating about what that meant for the safety of London.

This wasn't news to them, and the end of the trial was also why they were finally able to leave town. They'd given their sworn statements before the initial arrests but had been asked to remain in town in case they needed to testify in court for the trial. Because of the risk of mob retaliation, they were grateful they were never called to testify.

Margaret lifted the *Daily Express* paper lying in her lap and scanned the article Vic had written to see if the radio's news was accurate. Throughout the arrests and trial, Vic had been given priority for information because of his assistance with the case early on.

Vic's article said Billy Morton was sentenced to twelve years of imprisonment for conspiracy, extortion, and fraud. Eddie Holt received a ten-year term and was higher up in the organization than they had originally believed. Charles only received eighteen months since he did not realize he was working with the mob and his infractions were not as extensive as those in the mob family. Regardless of his awareness of who he worked for, he was still found guilty of conspiracy to defraud.

"How did your conversation with Charles go yesterday?" Margaret asked. Graham had met with Charles between the court hearing and waiting for the judge's verdict.

"Not well. I told him I'm sorry he's going through this, but it's a good chance for him to reevaluate things in his life. I also told him that I forgive him for his part in sabotaging my company." He took a hand off of the steering wheel and rubbed his face. "His response was that I didn't understand because I had everything given to me. He made the excuse that this was his chance to make it big, and he was well on his way until I ruined everything."

Margaret laid a hand on his shoulder. "I'm so sorry. You've worked hard to get where you are. You've also poured a lot into him over the years, spending time with him and pointing him to Jesus. We can pray that those seeds you planted will take root."

Graham nodded. "I also took him a Bible. It's one I'd been making notes in for him to guide him through and help him understand it. The warden took it and said I could leave it with the chaplain to give to him, so that's what I did. I guess they have to check it, so hopefully it will get back to Charles."

"Yes. We can pray about that, too, and that he'll begin to read it for himself."

"I still can't believe Charles was involved in all that—even if he didn't know they were the mob."

Though Margaret had never been close with Charles, she understood the sadness Graham felt over someone rejecting the things of God. "There's so much brokenness in the world. But in a way, God used it for good. Our company wouldn't be booming like it is if all this hadn't happened. Even with the extra staff we've hired, we're struggling to keep up with the number of authors coming to us. Forty-two additional authors from the list of one hundred is astounding."

"You're right. I should focus on the good that God is doing. He has blessed us."

Just before the arrests, Graham found out Hall & Wright had sent out letters to the list of one hundred, speaking ill of their legitimacy and saying they were stealing authors. Graham had filed a counterclaim for libel and damages against their lawsuit. Once the truth became publicly known, Hall & Wright wanted to settle quickly to clear their name. In the settlement, they agreed to send out a letter of retraction to each of the one hundred authors and to include advertising materials designed by Corbyn Publishing. Additionally, Hall & Wright gave Corbyn Publishing money to offset the monetary impact caused to their reputation by the lawsuit Hall & Wright filed publicly and their initial letters to the one hundred authors. The response to the new letters with their own advertising was overwhelming.

"Once the authors heard what kind of company this is, so many have wanted to be part of it, and I don't blame them. Your mission is what drew me in from the beginning." Margaret smiled at Graham as she recalled that first day in his office in the Belgravia house.

"You helped me make the mission clear. It's not just my mission anymore."

He reached over to squeeze her hand, and tingles shot up her arm.

"What time is your mother meeting us here?" Margaret had no idea what was scheduled for the day.

"I'd say we'll see her in half an hour or so."

"Oh. Should we . . ." Not that she didn't trust Graham, but she didn't want to sit in the house for half an hour alone with him. They had committed to keeping their relationship pure, and she didn't want to lay temptation in their path. "Maybe we should go get something from Ye Olde Shrieking Peach while we wait."

"We could do that. But I have something I want to show you in the garden first. We'll leave afterwards if you'd like."

"As cold as it is, I think that would be best." Though the late February temperature was well above freezing, she didn't relish standing around outside or even walking on the coast with the cold breeze. Instead, she imagined sipping a hot cup of tea while viewing the Channel from inside.

After pulling into the driveway and parking, Graham led Margaret to the garden. She was shocked to find a row of bright red rosebushes in large, elegant pots lining either side of the pathway to the door.

"Roses aren't in season." She glanced around at the dormant rosebushes in the garden. They looked like bushes of twigs. Her eyes flitted back to the living bushes. "Where did these come from?"

When she turned back to Graham, he was down on one knee, holding an open ring box. Tears rose to her eyes. It had been apparent their relationship was heading that direction, but she didn't expect it so soon. Yet with him before her, she couldn't imagine waiting much longer.

"Yes!" she squealed before he'd said a word, and he chuckled.

"What if I was just kneeling to pick something up from the ground?"

She placed a hand on her hip and faked a pout.

His smile grew. "Margaret Elliot, will you do me the honor of being my wife? I love you with all of my heart and want to spend the rest of my days loving you, cherishing you, and pointing you to God."

She leaned down and hugged him, her heart overflowing. "Yes to all of that. I love you, Graham."

"That makes me so happy." He kissed her on the cheek and lifted her as he rose. "You are the woman I have been waiting my whole life for. Together we are like Proverbs 27, where it says iron sharpens iron. You make me a better man and point me to God, and I want to spend the rest of my life doing that for you."

He released her and pulled a round solitaire diamond ring mounted in a platinum band out of a black velvet box labeled De Clare's. She gasped, recalling that De Clare's created jewelry for the Queen. He reached for her left hand and slid the ring on her finger.

"I can't wait to put the second ring on your finger."

In that moment, Margaret recalled the flash of the image that flitted through her mind the first day she met him. In that vision, she was staring up at him in front of a church with a pastor looking on. *God, thank you.* At the time, she didn't believe this was the life God had planned for her, but now she couldn't imagine anything different.

She also recalled Graham's more recent promised kiss and tilted her head up while staring into his gorgeous blue eyes. Joy danced across his face, and she briefly thought he would tease her. Instead, his look turned serious, and he leaned down to meet her.

When his lips finally touched hers, she melted into him and lost her balance. His arms wrapped around her and held her tight. It was every bit as dreamy as she'd imagined. After what seemed like an eternity, he lifted his head, but she couldn't bear the separation and pulled him back down. He didn't put up a fuss, and his kiss was as fervent as hers.

Eventually they did separate, and his hands slid down her arms to clasp her hands while his forehead met hers. "Are you ready to celebrate?"

She leaned back and tilted her head. "Celebrate?"

"Our mothers and siblings are here. And Katie."

"Here?"

He nodded in answer to her question.

"All of them?"

"Not all of the spouses. Most of them stayed back with the children. I hope you don't mind."

"Oh, my." She looked back at the house, examining the windows to see who might be watching, and several heads peeked around the edges. One of them stood out among the others—Katie's red head. Margaret's face flamed, but she laughed.

She wasn't used to being the center of attention around her sisters, but she'd gained much more confidence since she'd begun working with Graham. Like he said, they were good for one another, and she couldn't wait to see what else God had in store for them both.

Graham reached for her hand and tugged her back to him. "Before we go in, I'd like to pray over you and for our marriage."

She looked up and nodded.

"Our Heavenly Father, I thank you for the bountiful blessings you have bestowed on us. I thank you for Margaret. I am not worthy of such a gift, but I pray that you would guide me as I aim to lead our family. Show me how to love Margaret like Christ loves the church and to give myself up for her. Help us to seek you with all of our hearts that we might intertwine our lives with you and be a threefold cord, like in Ecclesiastes 4. Teach us to glorify you through our marriage. Show us how to take up the shield of the faith to quench the flaming darts of the evil one who would attempt to damage our marriage or our ministry. Now to you, Lord, who by the power at work within us is able to do far more abundantly than all that we ask or think, to you be glory in the church and in Christ Jesus to all generations, for ever and ever. Amen."

Her heart overflowed. This moment was better than she could have ever dreamed up for a book. She'd been searching for the perfect ending to her romance story . . . and she found it right here.

Chapter Twenty-Four

EPILOGUE

Three and a half years later
August 23, 1959

The trip to Mrs. Price's Kingsdown cottage had become as familiar to Margaret as the walk from their home to the office. Mrs. Price had been so kind as to let them borrow it for their third anniversary. Margaret twisted in the passenger seat for the umpteenth time to get comfortable. At six months pregnant, her body revolted at sitting still for too long. Nevertheless, she kept her complaints to herself, happy to have the time away from the busy office and spend a leisurely weekend with Graham.

He reached over and rubbed her belly before sliding his hand into hers and gracing her with one of his heart-melting grins.

"Is our little one making you uncomfortable?"

"I'll be okay. We're almost there." She slid their intertwined fingers to the top of her belly. "I hope it's a girl so we can name her Tracey after your sister."

"That would be nice. I know it would mean a lot to Mother."

"Not that I would mind if it's a boy and we named him after you. Graham is a good name."

He chuckled. "I'm glad you think so. I've always been happy with it. I'll be happy with whatever God blesses us with."

"I'd love a houseful like my mother had. Five or six children would fill our home with joy."

"I would love that. Again, I'll be happy with whatever God deems right for our family. We'll raise them to know the love of God and experience the joy of sharing him with the world."

"Yes, I want to leave that legacy." She pondered future children taking part in ministry work with them as they shared Jesus together. "And we'll raise them with a love of reading."

"That's a given. We can fill our home with a bookcase in every nook if necessary."

As they pulled around the bend in the road and came in view of the coast, she sighed. The weather was supposed to be perfect this weekend.

"Are you happy to be here?" Graham asked.

"I am. This cottage has become a place of respite. I'd love to get our own cottage here in Kingsdown someday. Though I will miss Mrs. Price's cottage. It holds many happy memories for us."

"I agree. It does hold happy memories."

"She's been so generous to let us stay here regularly. But I'm sure it gets tiresome for her, having others stay in her cottage."

"She has rarely used it over the past few years, and we do have it cleaned. Though you're right, I have felt like we're taking advantage of her generosity."

He pulled the car up just outside the gate of the cottage and motioned for Margaret to wait, then he hopped out and opened the gate so they could pull in.

The garden was in full bloom and set a dramatic backdrop for the cottage. She couldn't wait to clip the roses for bouquets to place throughout the cottage.

Before Graham came to help her out, she reached to the floorboard to retrieve a cream-colored leather satchel that held her gift for him. She didn't want him to accidentally see it. Even though it was wrapped, he would instantly have an idea of what it was.

"Your castle awaits, darling," Graham said as he reached for her hand.

"Why, thank you, my prince."

His eyes twinkled as he leaned down to capture her lips with his, and his free hand slid into her hair. She still found herself out of breath and off-kilter anytime he kissed her.

When he pulled back, he wrapped his hand around hers. "Do you want to lay that bag down? I can come back and get it with the luggage in a few minutes. I wanted to show you something first."

"Oh, no," she said teasingly. "I have something in here I don't want you to see yet."

"Well, now you have me so curious, I might try to sneak a peek." His mirth matched hers as he guided her through the garden path to the door.

When she shifted her gaze from him to the cottage, she noticed a bow and sign on the door. "What does it say? Did Mrs. Price leave us a note?" She looked back at Graham, and he shrugged.

As they drew nearer, she read, "'Welcome home.' I suppose it's starting to feel like a home to us, as much time as we spend here." They'd been here three times that summer alone. "The bow seems an unusual decoration for August though."

She looked up at Graham just as he leaned down and swept her into a bridal hold. She squealed in surprise.

"Happy anniversary, my love." He leaned in and pecked her on the lips.

"Happy anniversary to you too." This time, she leaned in and pulled him into a lingering kiss.

"Welcome to our very own getaway." He unlocked the door and set her down just inside.

She furrowed her brow. "Yes, we have this weekend as a getaway. Why did you say it like that?"

"Because this cottage is my anniversary gift to you. I bought it from Mrs. Price."

"What?" Margaret squealed in joy. "How . . . Did you really?" She looked around the cottage and noticed Mrs. Price's personal effects were gone, though the furniture and some accessories remained. "How did you manage that?" She opened the door and peeked back out to the garden. "All of this is mine . . . ours too?"

"Yes, and yes, the garden is mainly yours—you didn't misspeak. I know how much you adore it."

"Oh, thank you, thank you, thank you!" Margaret flung her arms around his neck and pulled him as close as her belly would allow. "What a treasure. I can't believe you kept a straight face when I said I wanted to get a cottage in the area."

"I can't believe I did either. I thought surely I would crack and you would guess."

"No, even when you were trying to tell me, I didn't understand. You had to spell it out. How did you convince Mrs. Price to sell it to you?"

Graham stepped back and slipped his hand into hers. "Let's go sit down in *our* parlor and talk."

Once they were seated together on the sofa, he turned to her. "I actually began asking her about a year and a half ago. At the time, she wasn't interested, but I restated my interest each time we came out to visit, and eventually she said she would think about it. She finally said she realized she rarely came here anymore. Her children live nearer Brighton, and when she goes to the coast, it's generally in that direction. I did promise her that if she or her children ever want to visit the Kingsdown area, they can stay here."

"I think that's quite reasonable."

"Yes. So here we are. A few months ago, she agreed, and I wanted to give it to you for our anniversary."

"When did you sign the papers?"

"A month ago."

"So the last time we visited . . ."

He grinned and chuckled. "Yes. This place was ours. But I had asked her not to remove her things so you wouldn't wonder what was going on. Though it is already ours, the only thing left is for you to add your signature. I'd like your name on it too. Otherwise, it doesn't feel like a gift."

"Of course you would." She smiled up at him and shook her head. "You're the same one who had me sign my name as co-owner of Corbyn Publishing when we returned from our honeymoon. Not many men would do such a thing. But then, I should know better. You're like no other man I know. I'm glad you're mine." She swung her arm around him and leaned in for a kiss.

When she released him, it took her a minute to come back to her senses. "I almost forgot." She reached for her satchel and pulled out the present. "If we're giving gifts now, I should give you yours, though it seems paltry compared to what you gave me."

"It's not about the size or cost of the gift. I'm sure it will be something of great meaning, knowing you."

Margaret bit her lip. It did hold great meaning.

She handed it to him, and he exclaimed, "A book is always a welcome gift." Unwrapping it revealed a leather-bound book. "A romance." He raised a brow.

Sitting up straight, Margaret recalled what she'd rehearsed. "It's leather-bound because that's the gift for third anniversaries."

"How thoughtful."

"There's more. Remember when I first saw you here after the mob attack? Before we were engaged?"

He nodded with a smile. "On this very sofa."

"And I told you I'd written a romance. This is it."

His brow furrowed. "I'd meant to publish it for you at the time. I'm sorry. I forgot all about it."

"I'm glad you forgot. It gave me a chance to surprise you. Frances edited it, and I had it printed secretly. It's not our love story, but there are pieces of ours in it. One day, maybe, we can publish it for the world. But right now it's ours."

He ran a hand through her hair and gazed at her softly. "And to think, that first day of work, you said you didn't write romance because you didn't know enough. I thought you were beautiful and wanted to right that wrong but never dreamed we had this beautiful future ahead of us. Is there enough romance in your life now?"

"I could write volumes now. But other than this one book, I think God has called me to write other things. But that doesn't mean we can't pretend I need to do romantic research."

He tugged her close and kissed her temple, then cheek. Her eyes drifted closed as he moved down to the corner of her mouth. He pulled back, and she opened her eyes, missing his lips.

Grinning, Graham said, "That was where I stopped the first time I kissed you on this sofa."

"But you don't need to stop now."

"No." His grin grew, and he shook his head. "There's no stopping me now." He leaned down again and found her mouth, and her heart leaped.

This was more than the life she'd imagined for herself—glorifying God in her work alongside the love of her life. This was truly living. She silently prayed that the seeds of the gospel that her family was planting would live on long after they were gone.

The End

What to read next: Have you read the rest of the Not Quite Series? Be sure to turn the next few pages to read about some of the other books in the series! Or you can find out more at KimGriffin.org

May the God of hope fill you with all joy and peace in believing,
so that by the power of the Holy Spirit you may abound in
hope.
    Romans 15:13 ESV

Afterword

When I first wrote Not Quite Mr. Darcy, I had no plans to make it a series, but God kept giving me stories that tied to one another. The thread through the entire Not Quite Series is Margaret Elliot Corbyn. She is a key but side character at the end of life in Not Quite Mr. Darcy. In Not Quite Colonel Brandon and Not Quite Mr. Knightley, Margaret is mentioned multiple times but never on the page. Because the main books in the series are all set after this 1955 prequel, Margaret's life and legacy of faith shine in the other books.

As I wrote this story, I intended it to be a challenge to myself and to you. What is the legacy that you will leave from the things you do now and throughout your life? As a Christian, I want my legacy to be one that points to Christ as Lord and Savior. It is my hope that this book and the entire series show you that you are never too young or too old to do great things for God's kingdom. Even things that seem small are big in God's economy. And what's more, if you are a Christ follower, know that if God has called you to step out and do something, He will equip you to do it. The God who created the universe by speaking it into existence has the power to do through you the seemingly impossible. Let this give you hope and encouragement. Matthew 19:26 ESV - But Jesus looked at them and said, "With man this is impossible, but with God all things are possible."

When I began this book, I was excited to tell the happy parts of Margaret's story, long before she succumbed with dementia. In some ways she represents my mom, who battled with Alzheimer's for fourteen and a half years before she went to be with the Lord. Margaret and my mom's lives are different in most other ways, but their love for God and desire to share Him is another similarity.

My mom loved to wear butterfly brooches, shirts, and other accessories for this very reason. She would tell people the butterflies represented new life in Christ. 2 Corinthians 5:17 ESV - Therefore, if anyone is in Christ, he is a new creation. The old has passed away; behold, the new has come.

While writing this story, I enjoyed adding in Margaret's best friend, Katie, who was mentioned in Not Quite Mr. Darcy. Showcasing their friendship was a highlight of the story, because I know firsthand how precious friendships in Christ are.

As God would have it, near the end of writing this story one of my mom's dearest friends, Miss Sherry, went to be with the Lord. I know they are surely celebrating in heaven. Meanwhile, her loss is tremendous. She was not only like a mother to me, but she leaves behind a daughter and granddaughters. Miss Sherry was like my mom in that she loved to share Jesus. She had a servant's heart and often served behind the scenes in a prayer ministry and in helping those in need.

Both my mom and Miss Sherry poured into me throughout my life, encouraging me to follow God's call, and both women left the kind of legacy I hope to emulate.

In the dedication, I mentioned Miss Sherry loved hummingbirds. Did you know that hummingbirds are not native to Great Britain and at the time of the story they would have only been found in places like a special collection at a zoo? In the U.S. they are quite common. Miss Sherry loved to put out her hummingbird feeders and flowers that attracted them.

Another theme of this story is following God's call even when it's hard, and from that comes the idea of doing what is right even when it costs something. Often when we are following God, opposition will come. There are many who have given their lives in following God's call.

Being raised in the U.S. at this time, that can seem so foreign, but there might come a time where standing up for what is right is just that costly.

In my books, I show people studying God's Word to understand His will and plan for their lives and to build confidence in Him. I hope that you will be driven to study His Word too. Knowing His word will help us discern what is right and true when people twist His words. If you want to know more about how to study scripture, reach out to me through my website: KimGriffin.org. I have been leading Bible studies for many years, and it is my heart's desire to help others study His word too. Until we see God face to face, studying God's word is the best way to know His truths.

To find out more about the making of this book, check out the extras page and follow the link to the special page on my website that's only with the special link on the Extras page.

Be sure to check out the Extras page for the link to the behind the scenes information.

Get a free novella: *Not Quite Mr. Tilney* (Katie's story) with newsletter signup at KimGriffin.org

Thank you for reading! May the words of this book be a blessing to you and point you to the One who loves you best—Jesus!

Extras

There are always stories behind the writing of my books and fun facts I find while researching, so I like to have an Extras page for each of my fiction books. Fun fact: This book was written and published the year of Jane Austen's 250th birthday!

If you have any of my other books, be sure to check out their extra pages too! It's something special I like to reserve for those who read them. You can access it through the QR code below or visit this link: https://www.kimgriffin.org/home/books/Extras-NQMA

If you enjoyed this book, don't forget to leave a review on Amazon, Goodreads, Bookbub or anywhere you review books.

Acknowledgments

I thank God for giving me words to write and placing this series on my heart. One of the things that drove me to write was reading books like Jane Austen's and wishing they had faith incorporated. Finding the love of our lives, while wonderful, does not fulfill our desire to be perfectly loved, because no man is perfect except Jesus.

My hope in each book in this series, and all of my fiction, is to point to Christ as the one who satisfies the longing of our hearts. May these books be to His glory.

I also thank God for placing people in my life like my mom and Miss Sherry, who pointed me to Him in my early years and helped me see through their lives what it means to serve God wholeheartedly.

Thank you, Dani Renee and Erica Dansereau, for Beta reading and helping me to craft this book into something lovely. And thank you to my editor, Heather Wood, for catching all of my typos and making this book so much better. All of you are amazing authors in your own right, and I'm so glad to walk this path with you and to be part of CMW with you.

Christian Mommy Writers, I am so thankful for you! You ladies spur on my writing, encourage my faith, and remind me that it's okay to have trouble juggling the mom (and now grandmother) hat alongside writing and other hats I wear. You are a gift from God.

Thank you, ARC Team for working hard to promote my book and for caring about this ministry that God has called me to. What a blessing to run this race alongside you.

Last but not least, I thank my husband and family for sharing me so I can write. I love you all!

Kim Griffin is a former interior designer and homeschool mom who has been leading Bible studies for over 35 years and working in Women's Ministry for over 25. Several years ago, God led her to begin writing words of hope. She writes Christian women's fiction with clean romance and devotionals/Bible studies. Her desire is that her books will draw readers closer to the God who sees all of their imperfections and loves them still.

If you enjoyed this book, please consider leaving a review on Goodreads and Amazon! As an independent author this helps Kim get the word out about her books.

You can learn more about Kim and her books and sign up for her newsletter at her website:

kimgriffin.org

Also by Kim Griffin

Scan the QR code to see my other books or visit KimGriffin.org

Scan this QR code to join my newsletter and receive a free novella: ***Not Quite Mr. Tilney***, and a free Gospel of John simple self-paced study guide. You'll also receive updates on my writing, book and author suggestions, discounts on books, freebies, and more!

NOT QUITE SERIES

Book 1

Book 2

Book 3

Book 4
Prequel

Book 4.5
Newsletter
Only
KimGriffin.org

Faith-centered romance series with
gentle nods to the works of Jane Austen
Twists & turns, mystery, love
1955 to present

Read more of the Not Quite Series

"It is a truth universally acknowledged, that Mr. Darcy does not exist."

Follow Kate's story of life after loss as she travels from Memphis, TN to coastal England to care for Margaret, a dementia patient

Available as an ebook & paperback.
Check website for retailers.
KimGriffin.org

A missionary, A pendant, Love

Join Megan's mystery while this
North Carolinian living in England
learns God's plan is more magnificant
than her own

Available as an ebook & paperback.
Check website for retailers.
KimGriffin.org

A runaway bride
A marriage of convenience
A love worth fighting for

Nancy's 1970 story of joy from shame displays how God sees us and loves us even in our brokenness

Kim's other books

Sometimes everything has to go wrong before we appreciate Mr. Right

Broken, Brooke moves to Kissimmee, Florida and finds herself, God, and love

Non-Fiction

Starry Night is a Christ-centered daily scripture reading and study for December 1-26. It looks at Christ in scripture: preincarnate in the Old Testament, prophecies, miracles and key moments in his life, and finally his birth with a hint of what's to come!

Available as an ebook, paperback, and hardcover. Check website for retailers.

KimGriffin.org